Combat
raced across the hotel lobby

He'd noticed the woman's interest in Brognola only a few seconds earlier, and had started making his way toward her when she'd pulled a weapon. Her hesitant movements had warned Bolan that she was one of the Huntsman alters—and an innocent.

She made the warrior just before she leveled the pistol at Brognola. She swiveled toward him, and for an instant she appeared to be undecided. Then the woman tried to fall back into a defensive stance and bring the pistol into target acquisition.

Launching himself at her the last few feet, the warrior caught the assassin around the waist in a flying tackle that dropped them both on the tiled floor. He straddled her and struck a blow that caught her wrist and sent the weapon spinning away.

"Striker!" Brognola yelled as he tried to clear his .38 from leather.

Then gunfire rang throughout the lobby.

Hammered backward, the big Fed crashed through the double entrance, shattered glass raining over his body.

MACK BOLAN ®

The Executioner

DON PENDLETON'S
EXECUTIONER®
ARMED FORCE

THE
ARMS
TRILOGY
★ BOOK III ★

A GOLD EAGLE BOOK FROM
WORLDWIDE.

TORONTO • NEW YORK • LONDON
AMSTERDAM • PARIS • SYDNEY • HAMBURG
STOCKHOLM • ATHENS • TOKYO • MILAN
MADRID • WARSAW • BUDAPEST • AUCKLAND

First edition May 1995
ISBN 0-373-61197-8

Special thanks and acknowledgment to
Mel Odom for his contribution to this work.

ARMED FORCE

The love of money is the root of all evil.

—1 Timothy, 6:10

Evil deeds do not prosper.

—*The Odyssey*,
Homer

Arming a warrior to fight against his enemies is an honest trade, but fomenting death and destruction for profit and gain is nothing short of evil. The predators should know that the devil always gets his due.

—Mack Bolan

THE
MACK BOLAN®
LEGEND

Nothing less than a war could have fashioned the destiny of the man called Mack Bolan. Bolan earned the Executioner title in the jungle hell of Vietnam.

But this soldier also wore another name—Sergeant Mercy. He was so tagged because of the compassion he showed to wounded comrades-in-arms and Vietnamese civilians.

Mack Bolan's second tour of duty ended prematurely when he was given emergency leave to return home and bury his family, victims of the Mob. Then he declared a one-man war against the Mafia.

He confronted the Families head-on from coast to coast, and soon a hope of victory began to appear. But Bolan had broken society's every rule. That same society started gunning for this elusive warrior—to no avail.

So Bolan was offered amnesty to work within the system against terrorism. This time, as an employee of Uncle Sam, Bolan became Colonel John Phoenix. With a command center at Stony Man Farm in Virginia, he and his new allies—Able Team and Phoenix Force—waged relentless war on a new adversary: the KGB.

But when his one true love, April Rose, died at the hands of the Soviet terror machine, Bolan severed all ties with Establishment authority.

Now, after a lengthy lone-wolf struggle and much soul-searching, the Executioner has agreed to enter an "arm's-length" alliance with his government once more, reserving the right to pursue personal missions in his Everlasting War.

PROLOGUE

Memphis, Tennessee

She stood in the shadows as she waited, dressed in soft corduroy slacks that were shoved into low-cut boots of matching black, and a teal-colored blouse under a black cotton vest. Her cropped auburn hair dropped into the collar of the fringed black leather jacket cut Western-style, which blocked the hint of a chill wind that blew in from the street. The deep purse slung over her right shoulder held the reassuring weight of a Glock 17.

The predators watched her from a lamppost half a block down the street. Their silhouettes cut into the soft neon glow of the run-down motel behind them. The three young men all wore similar clothing: jeans, T-shirts and motorcycle jackets crisscrossed with the silvered sheen of zippers. They moved their feet, and the clack of their rollerblade wheels striking the sidewalk reached her ears.

Only their hairstyles reflected any hint at individualism. The guy in the blue mohawk watched her intently. The second guy had a habit of flicking a lighter nervously, and the subdued radiance from the motel made his shaved head resemble a skull full of infection. The third guy, with a blond mane that reached to his shoulders, was obviously the leader.

The woman took her cue from him. Her senses were razor sharp. She realized almost as an afterthought that she might have run them in on general principles because they were a felony waiting to happen.

Then she wondered what she would have run them into. Quickly she stopped the line of thinking. She'd learned over the past few years that introspection like that would lead only to blinding headaches that would leave her bedridden at least for the next day. If she was still in the city come morning, she didn't want to miss work. The job at the radio station kept her cover in place.

She wished her contact would hurry. A glance at her watch told her he was already seventeen minutes late for the meet. If she'd had any input in the matter, she knew she would have already moved on.

Headlights crested the gentle rise at the end of the street. Instinctively she touched the key case hanging outside her purse that had the Vietnamese beer cap mounted on it. The key case was a source of comfort, though her car was parked seven blocks away.

The police markings on the driver's door turned incandescent amber as they caught the reflected light. The patrol car slowed, its brake lights flaring crimson for an instant.

The three predators tensed, their eyes locked on the police vehicle.

She shrank farther into the shadows and watched in grim anticipation. She felt the policeman hadn't seen her and was interested only in the three youths.

An instant later the taillights winked out and the police car sped up again. Apparently the close brush with law enforcement pushed the predators into a decision. They shoved away from the pole, their feet gliding across the uneven pavement.

She thought about the Glock 17 in her purse but rejected it until the pistol was necessary. There was no doubt they'd targeted her. Hard-edged moonlight gleamed in two fists, and she guessed they held knives to cut the shoulder strap of her purse.

Adrenaline surged through her as she squared off with them silently and stepped away from the building. For a moment she thought she heard a warning voice from deep inside her head. She ignored it. Her head was full of voices sometimes, and some of them never made any sense.

The predators were ten feet away and closing. "Drop the purse, bitch," the guy with the blue mohawk ordered. "You don't have to get hurt tonight."

Without saying anything, she reached into a nearby concrete planter and scooped out a double handful of white limestone rock. She slung it haphazardly on the sidewalk before her and listened to the sudden chorus of curses and yelps as the predators realized the danger that had been laid in front them.

The guy with the blue mohawk jerked and twisted like a mannequin dangling from the strings of an inexperienced puppeteer. Seizing her opportunity, the woman reached for the man and caught him in a hip throw. Pulling with all her strength, she yanked him airborne and hurled him at the plate-glass window fronting the building.

The glass broke in huge shards as the skater went through it with a frightened scream.

As she whirled away from the guy with the shaved head, she was aware of the knife blade clicking against her dangling hooped earring. She met the third man with a knee to the groin that drained all motor control from him in a heartbeat. Her hands came up defensively as her second victim dropped into a fetal curl a few feet away.

"Now you're going to get it, bitch!" the surviving predator promised. He stuck out a hand and went around the nearby light pole with an easy grace, the knife in front of him in a clenched fist.

She didn't wonder about her martial-arts skills as she confronted her attacker. Even though she couldn't remember specifically when, she knew she'd been surprised like this before. Reacting smoothly, she captured and controlled the knife hand as it licked out at her, then twisted and turned, flipping her assailant from his feet to land with a meaty thud on his back on the sidewalk. His breath whooshed out of him in an explosive gasp.

Regaining her feet, she hurried away from the scene. Out of her peripheral vision, she saw a dark green Lexus glide to a halt at the curb. The passenger door popped open, but the interior light didn't come on.

"Orchid," the man behind the steering wheel called, "get in the car."

Recognizing the code word, she sprinted for the vehicle, covering the distance in four long strides. She clambered inside and slammed the door.

The Lexus powered away from the curb. The man was intent on the rearview mirror. He was of medium height, with the broad shoulders and slim waist of a gymnast. "You were supposed to keep a low profile," he admonished as he took the first right turn he came to.

Still thrumming with adrenaline, she hugged herself and touched the key case, her thumb caressing the beer cap. At least a half dozen voices seemed to be clamoring for attention inside her skull. "Maybe we should have met in a better neighborhood."

The man glanced at her. "Are you all right?"

"For someone who was nearly killed," she said sarcastically, "I think I'm doing damn fine." Inside her mind, the voices were reaching fever pitch and she almost recognized some of them.

He checked the street, then looked back at her. "You don't look all right."

She closed her eyes and shook her head. "I'll be fine."

"Yeah." He didn't sound like he cared. Then, in a rougher voice, he said, "John Philip Sousa plays kazoo."

It felt as if a whirlpool opened up in her mind, a liquid vacuum that sucked all the voices away in a vortex of frightened passion. A door slammed shut. Only confidence and responsibility remained. She traced the surface of the key case again, lovingly. "There's an assignment?" she asked in a whisper.

"Yeah." The man retrieved a letter-size manila envelope from above the sun visor. "Guy named Harold Brognola down in Miami. Pictures are inside. He's a Justice Department agent heading up a special crime task force."

"My assignment?"

"Put him on a slab," the man replied.

The Huntsman opened the envelope and glanced through the pictures inside. They'd been shot through a telephoto lens that blurred out the details behind the man but left the target showing in extreme clarity.

"How soon?" the Huntsman asked, his personality filling up the vessel that had been the woman.

"You're on your way to the airport now. The sooner Brognola's dead, the sooner we all sleep better." The Huntsman tossed the envelope of pictures onto the dash and relaxed. He had his target firmly in mind now, and his skills made him as sure as the tracking system of a Tomahawk missile. Even if Brognola or his security people killed him, he'd only be reborn. He laughed, and didn't even think it odd that the emotion came out in a woman's voice.

1

"Drop site's coming up in four minutes."

Mack Bolan adjusted the harness strapped across his chest a final time, then stepped forward and hooked up to the night-black hang glider spread like a falcon's shadow across the cargo plane's interior. He thumbed the transmit button on his ear-throat headset. "We're ready, Jack."

"Roger." Jack Grimaldi was Stony Man Farm's chief wingman and had been cycled into the present operation with Bolan. "Satellite uplink shows we're all on target. Phoenix One has radioed that his ground control unit is in place and the exfiltration has been set up."

Bolan tested the hang glider's control bar, refamiliarizing himself with the feel of the aerial craft. "Affirmative. We jump on your go." The aluminum-and-cable frame felt heavy and solid, reassuring when he considered what he was about to do. He glanced at David McCarter, standing next in line.

The fox-faced Briton was ex-SAS and used to daring maneuvers. An accomplished pilot himself, he'd found a second home in the sky. The hang glider seemed to pose no problems for him.

Both Stony Man warriors were outfitted in blacksuits, their faces and hands masked by combat cosmetics. The Executioner carried the Beretta 93-R in shoulder leather and the heavy Israeli Desert Eagle .44 Magnum on his hip.

A cut-down Ithaca Model 37 12-gauge shotgun rode in a specially designed quick-release holster that ran from his right knee to his ankle. Extra magazines for the pistols and various other incendiaries were clipped to his combat harness, and a bandolier across his chest held extra shotgun rounds.

McCarter sported twin Browning Hi-Powers at shoulder and hip, and an H&K MP-5 SD-3 in a jackass sling across his back. He took a final puff from the cigarette he'd been smoking, then dropped it to the metal flooring of the cargo plane and crushed it underfoot.

"One minute," Grimaldi called out.

Bolan moved toward the rear of the plane as the aft hatch started to open with a grinding of gears. The metal halves parted to reveal a night sky holding only a fistful of bright stars, and the shadowy mountainous terrain thousands of feet below. Slitting his eyes against the wind, he leaned against the scarecrow frame of the heavy-duty motorized winch mounted beside the cargo door. With effort, he could make out the twin silver streams that were the railroad tracks they'd vectored in on. The spur line snaked into the foothills of the Abruzzi Apennines.

Somewhere ahead of them was the privately owned train carrying Calvin James and Sally Coleman to the Bloody Wind terrorist stronghold Aaron Kurtzman had turned up with the Farm's computers. Once they'd uncovered the connections to Alexander De Moray and Hayden Thone, the spider web linking various terrorist groups across the globe had become a little clearer. The Stony Man teams still weren't sure of the entire operation because not all of the cards were on the table. But Kurtzman had turned up the stronghold while researching Thone's munitions corporation. Fortress Arms, though now based in California instead of Germany, had a four-hundred-year history of dealing weapons. As a result of those dealings, it had acquired a number of holdings. The stronghold in the Italian mountains was only one of them.

Calvin James had gone missing from Phoenix Force during an attempt to free Rear Admiral Coleman's daughter after she was kidnapped during the hijack of American arms that had been transferred from a closed military base to the Italian army. American and Italian military personnel were still scouring the countryside looking for the munitions and the rear admiral's daughter. Price and Kurtzman had turned up the probable location of the Bloody Wind hardsite, confirmed it surreptitiously through CIA files without tipping their hand to anyone at Langley, and given the information to the Executioner and Phoenix Force with the President's blessings.

"Thirty seconds." Grimaldi's tone was easy, relaxed. He'd delivered the Stony Man hard corps all over the globe. "You guys are going to have bare seconds to get clear," he reminded them, "before this ungainly goose goes beyond my control at this altitude."

The cargo plane hadn't been designed for acrobatic maneuvers, but it had the necessary tail doors for freight entry that had been required by Bolan's choice of tactical deployment. The train's current speed was roughly thirty miles an hour, and the mountain terrain terraced by brush and pockets of forest on either side of the tracks didn't allow for even 4WD vehicles. Any forced stop would have given the Bloody Wind terrorists the chance to kill James and Sally Coleman.

Bolan pulled his infrared goggles into place. Immediately the terrain shifted into a mixture of blacks and iridescent greens. He took the control bar firmly in both fists and braced himself.

"Okay," Grimaldi said, "we're in the loop. On my go. Counting down now." The plane nosed down in a steep dive. "Five, four—"

At zero, the cargo plane leveled out. Bolan maintained his stance with difficulty, feeling the much cooler air whip in around him. He grabbed hold of the winch and kept himself upright.

Grimaldi relayed the tactical Intel. "Okay, gentlemen, you're at four hundred feet plus. The train is less than a thousand yards ahead of you. The Bear confirms that we haven't been spotted as yet because there's been no response inside the train."

Bolan knew the Stony Man computer teams were monitoring the situation through the thermal-imaging capabilities of a military satellite 22,000 miles out in space. The train consisted of a locomotive, a coal car and two old passenger carriages that contained wooden benches. Capable of peering through the wooden walls of the passenger carriages with infrared, Kurtzman and his team had confirmed that James and the rear admiral's daughter were being held in the first passenger car. The Stony Man intelligence team was also monitoring the radio chatter between the train crew and the station operator based at an old coal mine at the end of the spur.

"On my go," Grimaldi said. The cargo plane's engines sounded throaty and strong in the empty hold.

"On your go," Bolan said, and McCarter echoed him an instant later.

Abruptly the cargo plane twisted on its tail, reaching for the sky and sunfishing like a bull in a rodeo event.

Bolan was almost knocked from his feet and struggled against the sudden shift in gravity. The hang glider rustled and billowed as the wind rolled in under it. He kept his attention riveted on the stern opening. Through the lenses of the infrared goggles, the terrain spun dizzily.

The cargo plane's engine's coughed and died, and the steep climb it had started came to a halt. For a moment everything seemed weightless.

"Now!" Grimaldi called.

Powering himself forward, the Executioner headed for the tail opening. His sense of balance was almost useless, confused by the sudden inertia of the plane. McCarter was at his heels. The warrior shot between the gaping jaws of the doors and into the churning wind outside the plane. A shrill zip captured his attention, and he swiveled his head in time to see the fabric covering the hang glider's sail tear slightly as it skated past the top half of the cargo door. The damage appeared minimal.

Plunging downward to avoid any possible contact with the cargo plane, Bolan arced his body in a straight line. He aligned himself with the sail, feeling the chill wind whip across his face. He fell almost fifty feet before trying to achieve control over the descent. Gradually he pulled back on the control bar and felt the sail fill. Within seconds, he'd gone from falling to flying.

He pulled back farther, gaining altitude and getting a momentary view of the cargo plane. Grimaldi had pulled it out at almost treetop level, skimming above oak trees, chestnuts and olive trees as he vanished to the west.

"He's got it, mate," McCarter said. "Pretty bit of flying."

"Thanks," Grimaldi radioed back.

"Okay," the warrior said. "Let's make the jump to the alternate frequency." He reached up and switched the headset over. Focused on the laboring train below and ahead of them, he adjusted the hang glider's approach accordingly. He could tell at once that they were eating up the distance separating them. "Copy?"

"Copy," the Briton replied.

"Stony Base copies, as well," Kurtzman's deep voice rumbled. "Stand by for the patch-through to tactical ops."

Bolan took the time to glance to either side for McCarter. He found the man on the leeward side, slightly higher than his own position. The Phoenix warrior's hang glider resembled a giant black kite sailing across the star-filled sky. Resettling his grip, the Executioner pushed forward and dropped altitude. The incline had slowed the train further, and the hang gliders were easily doing more than twice its speed.

The headset crackled.

"Stony Base to Phoenix One," Kurtzman said.

"Phoenix One is standing by." Yakov Katzenelenbogen was a onetime Mossad agent who'd seen some of Israel's bloodiest action before joining Stony Man Farm's international strike force team.

"Phoenix Four," Kurtzman continued.

"I'm in the loop." Rafael Encizo had learned the arts of death in his Cuban homeland in a resistance group that worked against Castro and communism. He still bore the scars of his training and a stay in El Principe prison before linking up with Phoenix Force.

"Phoenix Three copies, too," a deep voice added. Gary Manning had a talent with anything possessing an explosive nature.

"Okay, Striker," Kurtzman said, "we're all in."

"Affirmative, Stony Base," Bolan replied. "We're on final approach. Out." The warrior made more adjustments to the hang glider. The intervening distance had dropped to less than sixty yards and was continuing to decrease quickly.

"I'm on target, mate," McCarter radioed.

Bolan glanced at the Briton, who soared as gracefully as a butterfly, slightly below and behind him now. He focused on his own target zone, the control bar cold in his gloved fists.

The hang glider knifed through the air. The warrior dropped the altitude to less than fifteen feet above the lead passenger carriage. Below him, the train flowed like a jerking steel river. The pulling unit was less than a football field away from the last rise they'd chosen as the outer edge of the envelope for the insertion. Bolan heard the doomsday numbers click into place in his mind.

"Phoenix Two?" the warrior said. He peered down, trying to match his speed as closely as he could to the train. He had to gain altitude momentarily to do it.

"In place."

Bolan shoved the control bar forward again, dropping down. "Let's get it done."

"Striker," Kurtzman called, "looks like two guys are going topside for a smoke."

"Roger." The Executioner cut the hang glider's harness loose and dropped. He was dimly aware of it continuing to sail forward, then disappearing in a tangle of trees as the train lumbered onward. His knees bent to absorb the impact, he landed atop the moving passenger carriage with his arms thrust out to balance himself. The landing was harder than he'd anticipated, and he had to roll to prevent breaking an ankle.

Awkward to a degree because of the munitions strapped to his combat harness—and moving in a different direction than the train—he rolled dangerously close to the passenger carriage's edge. The clacking as the train passed over the rails drowned all other sounds. Then he ran out of surface and tumbled over the side of the passenger carriage. Flailing out, he caught the edge of the car with both hands and halted his fall. The metal ridge bit into his fingers.

"Striker," McCarter called.

"Still with you," Bolan replied. He hauled himself up to chin-level, then threw a leg over the edge of the car as the two men came into view.

Both were dressed in khaki and carried AK-47s slung over their shoulders. The shorter man held a flame cupped between his palms while his companion leaned in with a cigarette.

Less than twenty feet away, Bolan watched the man's eyes widen in surprise as he spotted the warrior. The terrorist spit out his cigarette, scattering a string of orange coals as it bounced away. He went for his weapon, screaming out a warning.

Rolling over and coming to a halt on his stomach, Bolan freed the Ithaca Model 37 from the improvised boot scabbard and thumbed off the safety.

The terrorist had unslung the assault rifle and was firing. A line of ragged holes punched through the roof of the passenger carriage, eliciting sudden screams from below.

Drawing target acquisition on the center of the terrorist's chest, the Executioner took up trigger slack. The shotgun boomed, throwing out a tight pattern of 12-gauge buckshot that plucked the terrorist from the roof and hurled him over the side of the train.

The sudden flare of autofire turned the infrared goggles milky with aftereffects, rendering them useless.

Bolan fired blind, trusting his combat senses, loosing the first blast, then racking the slide and moving slightly to the right to track the guy's probable defensive movement before unleashing the second round. Steel splinters from the carriage's rooftop spiked into his left cheek, but the assault rifle's roar faded.

He swept the goggles away, dropping them into his chest pack in case he needed them later, then pushed himself to his feet and raced for the forward end of the passenger carriage. He blinked twice to clear his vision. Autofire from the other end of the second passenger car let him know McCarter had run into troubles of his own.

After thumbing fresh shells into the shotgun's magazine tube on the run, the Executioner swung over the side and started down the ladder leading to the observation platform below. A terrorist brandishing an Uzi leaned out of the door. He didn't see the big warrior until the Ithaca's muzzle pushed into his throat. When the terrorist recoiled in desperation, the Executioner fired from point-blank range.

The shotgun charge hammered the man from the doorway. The Uzi stuttered briefly, then was silent as it tumbled from the corpse's fingers.

Still on the move, Bolan swung down to the platform and took up a position inside the door. Tapping the headset's transmit button, the warrior said, "Phoenix Two."

"Go."

"I've got the door."

"Take it. That's me coming from the other way as soon as I finish placing the charges."

Bolan stepped through the door, aware of the gunfire echoing around the passenger carrier and the harsh screams coming from inside the coach. He leveled the Ithaca in both hands.

Illumination inside the car was dim, leaking from a string of low-wattage bulbs hanging naked from the wooden ceiling. The weak yellow glow spilled over the seven occupants. Calvin James and Sally Coleman were toward the back to the Executioner's right, out of the line of fire. Two terrorists guarded the back door with compact machine pistols. Another man stood at James's side, holding an AK-47 butted against his hip and screaming orders at the other men. The fourth man was staring out the window on the right, looking back to see what all the commotion was about. The fifth terrorist lunged at Bolan, screaming a warning as he aimed his pistol.

Reacting instantly, the Executioner slapped the threatening pistol away with the shotgun barrel. He slipped his hand free of the trigger, fisted the man's clothing and slammed him through the door toward the low railing that run around the observation deck.

A surprised cry ripped from the man's lips before he tumbled over the side and disappeared.

The hardman closest to him wheeled away from the large sliding window and brought up an IntraTec 9 mm pistol in a scarred fist.

Bolan extended the Ithaca in both hands and squeezed the trigger. The 12-gauge boomed in the enclosed space. A tight knot of pellets caught the terrorist in the chest and bounced him from the wall.

Knowing the doomsday numbers had trickled down to nothing, the Executioner racked the Ithaca's slide and chambered a fresh shell. The headset buzzed in his ear.

"Fire in the hole!" McCarter warned.

A heartbeat later, the train shuddered as the C-4 charges went off.

Managing his balance with difficulty, Bolan moved the shotgun's path from the man beside James to the men at the rear of the passenger carrier. The terrorist leader had ducked toward the Phoenix Force warrior, taking cover as he unleashed a preliminary burst from the Russian assault rifle that raked splinters from the door frame by Bolan's head.

As the man on the left whirled, the machine pistol in his hand taking out the windows on the hellfire warrior's right, the Executioner fired again. The 12-gauge charge took the gunner in the chest and flattened him against the wall. Bolan had racked the slide before the corpse fell to the floor.

"The other car's been sheared loose," McCarter radioed. "Your situation?"

"Stay out," Bolan replied.

"You got it, mate. I'm starting forward across the rooftop."

Bolan dived behind the nearest seat. He'd seen Calvin James come surging up from his position to attack the terrorist leader and prevent the man from pointing his weapon at the screaming young woman beside him.

The corner of the seat was chopped away by a hail of bullets. Then the vinyl jumped as more rounds tunneled their way through the seat seeking the Executioner's flesh. Bolan slid to the floor and drew his Desert Eagle. It felt hard and sure in his hand as he rolled into the opening between the double row of seats.

James, hands cuffed in front of him, pushed the Bloody Wind terrorist like a linebacker closing on a quarterback. The terrorist was propelled backward, his rifle chattering away.

The surviving terrorist against the back door had fed a fresh clip into his weapon and spotted Bolan. He wheeled behind his own seat.

The Executioner looked under the row of seats and located the terrorist's bare ankle above the leather sandal. He sighted carefully, then dropped the Desert Eagle's hammer. The gun cracked and jumped in his hand. Packing power and mass, the bullet slammed into the hardman's ankle and almost amputated the foot. The guy didn't have time to yell as he was knocked to one side.

Bolan followed up with two rounds immediately, scoring on the man's head both times. Moving toward Sally Coleman, he shifted so he could cover James and the closed door he'd come through.

The Phoenix Force warrior had pressed to his advantage the initial surprise he'd garnered. Holding his cuffs on either side of the terrorist's face, he used the short length of chain between them to catch the man under the chin and shove his head through one of the large windows. Glass splintered, then blew away. The AK-47 cycled dry as James grabbed the terrorist by the hair with both hands. Before the man could free himself, the ex-SEAL dragged his throat across the broken shards of glass remaining in the window. With a cold look locked on his dark features, James threw the dying man through the window.

"Company's coming," McCarter transmitted.

"Affirmative," Bolan replied. He helped Sally Coleman to her feet and looked at James. "The cuff key?"

"There." The Phoenix Force warrior pointed as he scooped up an Uzi, then thrust a Beretta 92-F into his waistband.

Pulling the woman after him, Bolan reached the dead man James had indicated and went through the guy's pockets. He turned up the key in short order, uncuffed Sally Coleman and tossed it to James. The second set of handcuffs thudded to the wooden floor seconds later.

Bolan tapped the transmit button on the headset. "Striker to Phoenix One."

Katz's reply was almost instant. "Go."

"What's your location?"

"We're en route, perhaps minutes away."

"Resistance?"

"No."

Bolan opened the door cautiously. The wind whipped into his face, chill and threatening. Only a few feet away, the coal car jerked and clacked across the tracks. "Phoenix Two?"

"Here, mate. Best pull your head back inside. I'm blowing the coupling in just a moment."

The pack of C-4 plastique lay across the coupling and was held in place by Velcro straps already cut for that purpose. Before the Executioner could pull back, movement atop the coal car drew his attention. The heads of two terrorists came into view.

"You've got company," the warrior growled over the headset.

A blaze of small-arms fire thunked into the passenger carrier's roof, searching for McCarter.

Lifting the Ithaca, Bolan fired and racked the slide through all five rounds in the tube. The double-aught buckshot slammed into the chunks of coal, turning them into pebbles, dust and gray smoke that stained the night sky. The Executioner thought he might have scored on one of the targets but he couldn't be sure. They were racing the clock now. He withdrew into the passenger carrier and tapped the transmit button. "Blow it."

"Done," McCarter said. A series of explosions rippled through the night, stirring up vibrations that ran the length of the passenger carrier. "We've separated, mate, but there's still some trouble."

"What?" Bolan felt the passenger carrier slow, then come to a halt and start the drift back down the incline. He thumbed shells into the shotgun.

"I didn't get the chance to place the heavier charges along the coach's framework. The bloody thing's still intact."

"They can come after us."

"Right."

"Keep me posted."

"Always."

Bolan turned to James and passed him the extra headset he'd carried in his chest pack. The ex-SEAL had a dirty bandage over his side showing through the open shirt he wore, but looked none the worse for wear. Sally Coleman hovered at his side, taking comfort from his presence. "I'm going outside. Katz and Gary will be along shortly in ground transport. Until then, see if you can provide some cover fire and keep the lady safe."

"You got it." James took control of his charge and moved her to a corner of the coach car. At his urging, she sat down and partially covered her head with her hands and arms. Frightened tears were streaming down her face, but she seemed responsive and not paralyzed.

"Stony Base to Striker," Kurtzman called.

"Go." Bolan reached the back door of the car and peered through. Less than two hundred yards back down the tracks, the gutted hull of the rearmost passenger carrier was spread over the railway and parts of the countryside. Flames chewed into brush and hung from tree branches in fiery streamers. At their present rate of speed, they were going to slam into the wreckage in less than a minute. Even at a slow speed, the impact was going to be considerable.

Kurtzman went on calmly. "I wanted you to know the communications ops in the locomotive got off a message to the hideout. You've got troops already headed your way."

The mental map he'd formed of the territory took shape in Bolan's mind. At best, the main thrust of the Bloody Wind terrorists were ten minutes away. They had time, but it was going to be cutting the exfiltration close.

"Affirmative, Stony Base. We've got our people secured and are pulling up stakes here." The Executioner stepped out to the rear observation deck and onto the railing to grab the edge of the roof.

Perspiration covered the warrior, and when he reached the top of the coach car, the whipping wind cooled him. Behind, he could already see the flaming debris of the exploded car getting closer, yawning through the fire like the mouth of some amusement-park ride. Impact was imminent. He stayed low, covering the distance to the front of the passenger carrier in an easy jog. Occasional gunfire cracked but nothing came close.

McCarter lay prone on the rooftop, peering through a pair of night-vision goggles. "There's Katz." He pointed.

Bolan followed the line the Briton indicated and saw a pair of headlights coming down the mountainside from the wooded crest. Manning and Katz were driving a Land Rover they'd purchased from a nearby village, using it to transport the exfiltration gear. The Phoenix Force warriors were too far away to be any kind of help soon.

Rolling over, McCarter glanced at the wreckage behind them. "Would have been nice if that bloody thing had blown clear of the tracks."

"Dig in," Bolan said. "We'll have to try to ride it out. We've got enough bulk on our side that the impact could be less than we think." The wrecked coach car was less than seventy yards away. Their speed had picked up dramatically. The warrior lay down and took a firm grip on the passenger carrier's edge. The collision was only seconds away.

"They got the engine reversed," McCarter said.

Bolan glanced forward and saw that the locomotive and coal car were coming back at them. Along the uneven ridge of coal and hanging from the sides of the car, more than a dozen Bloody Wind terrorists were firing controlled bursts that chipped into the front of the disconnected passenger carrier.

Then the two coach cars slammed into each other, and the searing heat and the shrieks of tortured metal filled Bolan's senses.

2

Los Angeles

"You have a phone call, sir."

Hayden Thone glanced up from his guests as they sat at the umbrella-covered table outside the exclusive country club outside Los Angeles proper. Of the three people he shared the table with, the man and one of the women were film stars. The other woman, a keen-faced redhead, was a contact of his. She'd once been with the CIA, keeping tabs on munitions transfers throughout the NATO network.

Thone and the woman had carefully negotiated a deal for information while operating around the two movie stars out to impress each other and everyone around them. No one had noticed their exchange of identical valises while at the table, nor had anyone paid attention to the innuendo that had set up the switch.

With a look of expectation, the young waiter held out a cellular phone in an ornate box.

"Thank you," Thone said, "but I'd prefer to take it inside."

"Yes, sir."

Thone dropped a five-dollar bill into the phone box and got up. Dressed in white silk shorts that reached almost to his knees and a midnight-blue, collarless polo shirt, looking tan, fit and trim, he knew he had the attention of most of the ladies in the outside dining area.

Eyes hidden behind bronze-tinted aviator sunglasses, Thone checked the dining crowd for any signs of undue interest while he followed the waiter into the clubhouse. He knew from his contacts and the action that was currently taking place in Italy that his cover was dangerously close to being blown. Soon people would be hunting him, not just the Huntsman.

Inside the country club people were standing at the polarized windows enjoying the respite from the unaccustomed heat that had swelled over Southern California.

He took the call at a bank of private phones after getting the switchboard operator's attention and giving his name. Running his hand through his gray-flecked, short sandy hair, he checked his surroundings and found two men in dark suits that didn't fit in with the club's regular clientele. A sixth sense he'd developed early on in his career of gunrunning under his paternal grandfather snapped to attention.

"Thone," he said into the mouthpiece.

"It's me," Alexander De Moray answered. The Cajun was ex-Special Forces, ex-CIA and now Fortress Arms's invisible enforcer. He was also the core model for the Huntsman program. "Can you talk?"

"Where are you?"

"In Miami. In my car."

A mobile phone was easily tapped and wasn't as protected under the law as regular phone lines. "No," Thone replied. "I'll call you back at the office as soon as I can. Wait for me there."

"Right." De Moray broke the connection, leaving the empty static of white noise.

Cradling the receiver, Thone motioned to the waiter. When the young man came over, he said, "I have to go, but my friends will be staying behind. Please make sure they have everything they need and put it on my tab."

"Yes, sir."

Smiling brightly, Thone returned to his table and excused himself, saying he had to make a lengthy call and would be back soon. He took the valise from under the table when he left. Out of the corner of his eye, he saw Marilyn Haber get up to join him. Her arm was tense when she ran it through his.

"Trouble?" she asked.

The woman had worked in the field for some years, and Thone knew from his research of her that she could be dangerous in a physical encounter.

"I think so. There are two men watching us. Or you. Or me. I'm not sure." Thone continued walking casually, then turned his head to kiss the woman on her cheek.

"The suits?"

"Yes."

She looked at him and smiled. "They're watching you, love. So I think I'll be about my business."

"How very kind of you," he said dryly. "Do you know who they are?"

"No."

"Hazard a guess?"

She came to a stop and embraced him like a lover, which they'd never been. Pleasure all too often got in the way of business. "I'd say military. Probably intelligence boys."

"Why?"

"Their haircuts. The way they keep their gig line."

"Gig line?" Thone hugged her in return.

"The way they keep their belt buckle, tie and jacket buttons all in a line." Haber broke their embrace. "Also their tans. Those didn't come from a tanning booth and expensive oils. I'd say they've been exposed to the elements through their workday and not their intention. They still have a tint of red under them." She looked at him. "Any reason why military intelligence would be interested in you?"

"If so," he said evenly, "it's news to me." It wasn't exactly the truth. He'd taken some hits on undisclosed arms shipments around the world by a covert American group he'd almost run to ground. Once he knew who they were, and where, he'd be able to mount an offensive of his own.

She slipped a pair of dark sunglasses from her purse and put them on. Then she gave him a final kiss on the lips and said in a low voice, "I'm going to be careful for a few weeks to see if any of this rubs off on me. If it doesn't, and you're still in business, we'll see if there's another project we can work together on." Without another word, she walked away from him, her hips swaying seductively under the clinging yellow dress.

Thone didn't pause to watch her go. He moved quickly, walking toward the dressing room at the back of the country club. Checking the reflections in the windows of the pro shop in the center of the building, he saw the two men following him closely.

He turned left at the last intersection and passed into the dressing room. Showers hissed, and the low rumble of male conversation filled his hearing. He nodded to three men he was acquainted with, then stopped in front of his locker.

The two men in suits came in behind him, obscured for a moment by the curtain of steam coming from the shower area. They didn't see Thone.

The Fortress Arms CEO moved without hesitation. Keying the lock pad, he opened his locker door and reached inside with his free hand. He glanced around the row of lockers and saw the two men openly displaying IDs that got instant attention from the people they questioned.

A skinny guy in paisley boxers that Thone recognized from the golf course pointed in Thone's direction.

The club had laws about weapons. However, Thone had been a member for more than fourteen years, helping find the seed money for the club and working out the kinks in the real-estate problems. While others were searched occasionally, he never had been.

The red-and-gold gym bag held business articles he would need once he went into hiding. He shrugged the strap over his shoulder and unzipped a side pocket on the bag as the two men approached him. The specially silenced H&K squeeze-cocker with personalized grips filled his hand.

"Are you Hayden Thone?" The man who addressed him was in his early fifties, his reddish hair styled in a buzz cut. His chest was thick and broad, squared under his shoulders.

The other man was easily fifteen years his partner's junior. His face was hard and chiseled, a flushed tan around his mirror sunglasses, the small scar on his right cheek a livid white. He stood at parade rest, a good three inches over six feet.

"I'm Thone."

"I'm Major Michael Kennedy, military intelligence. I've got a few questions I'd like to ask you."

"Could I see your ID?"

"Sure." Kennedy flipped open the card case he carried, displaying the official documentation.

Thone peered at it long enough to see that the picture was a fair representation. Then he squeezed the H&K pistol three times in quick succession, shooting through the gym bag.

The intelligence man stumbled backward, propelled by the Glaser Teflon-and-shot combo bullets. His chest seemed to come apart, letting Thone know there'd been no Kevlar vest under the shirt.

The other man ducked with a curse, reaching for a weapon holstered under his jacket. His free arm flared out at Thone, trying for his gun arm.

Sidestepping fluidly, Thone batted his attacker's arm away with the valise as men started shouting around the dressing room. Without feeling, he shoved the H&K's barrel against the military intelligence officer's head and pulled the trigger.

Without a sound, the man died and jerked to the floor, knocking over the chrome-and-vinyl covered bench in front of the lockers.

Thone shoved the H&K into his shorts pocket as he headed for the door. A quick search through another compartment of the gym bag netted him the flip phone he kept there. He opened it and punched in a two-digit code as he went through the door. No one tried to stop him.

"Sandison," a rough voice with an Australian accent answered on the second ring.

"Is the helicopter ready?" The gun in Thone's pocket appeared to go unnoticed by the clientele standing in the halls, but he was aware of the dressing room door opening behind him.

"No, sir, but I can get it that way."

"Do it. We need to leave in a hurry. And make sure no one stops you. There might be some who try."

"Yes, sir."

Thone closed the phone and dropped it back into the bag.

"Someone stop him!" a voice shouted. "He just killed two people in here!"

A security man in a burgundy staff shirt and black slacks turned from his position near the rear exit doors. He was young and massive. He pointed at Thone and mustered a deep voice that might have been impressive to the two young women he'd been talking to. "Hey, you. Hold up a minute." He took a step forward as the girls backed away from him.

Without breaking stride, Thone drew the pistol from his pocket and fired through the rest of the clip. The special Glaser rounds cored into the man, stitching him from crotch to chin.

The security man jerked backward heavily and smashed through one of the large glass walls. Diamond-bright chips scattered around his corpse when he landed.

Thone hit the release bar with his elbow while he fit a fresh magazine into the H&K. He tripped the release, and the slide chambered the top shell with a metallic snap.

A small knot of men and a few women followed in his wake, but none made the effort to close the distance to less than twenty yards. He walked deliberately because he knew jackals got braver if a lion started to run.

Mentally he was already preparing a list of losses he had incurred the instant he shot the first military intelligence officer. The shooting range in L.A. would be gone, of course, as would most of the financial holdings in his name. But the majority of his wealth wasn't in the United States anyway.

The sleek Bell helicopter was waiting for him on the helipad, trimmed out in bright gold and green as black rotors fanned the air and sent dust devils scurrying across the hot tarmac. Sandison looked crisp and efficient at the controls, threatening with the mini-Uzi brandished openly in his fist.

Thone passed through the open door and took his place in the copilot's seat. "Go."

With a short nod, Sandison tucked away the mini-Uzi and worked the chopper's controls smoothly. The helicopter leaped into the air, leaving a milling crowd gathering below. "You seem to be the belle of the ball, mate."

"For the moment." Thone scanned the country club's grounds. There were three other helicopters on the helipad. All were stationary. Pursuit would be a while in coming. Thone quickly added the helicopter to his mental tally of losses. "We need to lose the chopper."

Sandison nodded. "Where?"

"The closest beach. I'll need to arrange ground transport." Thone took the flip phone from his bag.

"I take it we're hot," the pilot said as he made the necessary adjustments.

"Perfectly incendiary apparently." Thone punched in the first number from the list he'd memorized on his way out of the country club. The connection started ringing in short bursts.

"What about me?" Sandison asked. "They'll pull my license from the records on this crate."

"Disappear. Leave a message with Saint Olson's office in Zurich. I'll be in touch." Thone strapped the seat belts, finishing at the same time the phone was answered.

"Clay Pigeons." Salvatore Mancuso had helped Thone change the arms company's name from the original Festung Armor to Fortress Arms during the move in 1980 from Germany to California. The Sicilian had been instrumental in laundering the money Thone had made from illegal-arms dealings across an international market and in financing the shadow networks behind dozens of terrorist factions around the globe.

"Time to close down shop there," Thone said without preamble.

Mancuso's words were uninflected. "I've got some business dealings going on."

"Downstairs?"

"Yes. The group of Rastafarians from New York."

"I remember." Clay Pigeons wasn't just the premier shooting gallery in and around L.A., and didn't just cater to media stars by providing security, secrecy and hands-on training with a number of different weapons. It was also a clearing house for many of the arms deals Thone put together. Underground vaults held the weapons for a brief time before different buyers took delivery. Access tunnels to a car dealership two blocks southeast and a video-rental store to the north—held by companies owned by Thone under a corporate name Mancuso had established—provided delivery points.

"What do you want me to do about the Rastafarians?" Mancuso asked.

"Who's working the deal?"

"Vannick."

Thone studied the skyline in front of them. "Vannick's expendable. Burn him. Crash the computer system and get the hell out. Do it now."

"Of course."

Thone broke the connection. His next call was to an emergency driver he kept on twenty-four-hour standby. Danny Goss had been schooled in antiterrorist driving in Italy, and had been working for one of the primary shipping magnates when Thone had lured him away. Goss had no problem with meeting them at the beach despite the head start the helicopter had.

His next call went out overseas. Paolo Spada was a contact man he used for the Bloody Wind group working the arms shipment out of Rome. Although the terrorists didn't know they had a Huntsman alter in their midst, near the top of their organization, they were still following Thone's plans. Spada monitored the various spying devices the Huntsman alter in the Bloody Wind had placed in their retreat.

Spada answered on the sixth ring, irritating Thone. "I want to know the status of the American agent and the rear admiral's daughter," the munitions broker demanded in Italian.

"That's hard to say," Spada replied. "A covert force has attacked the train carrying both those people to the Bloody Wind stronghold. I'm trying to sort through the details now."

"Find out. Then get back to me." Thone rang off and looked at Sandison expectantly.

The pilot shrugged. "Eight, maybe nine minutes. I'm monitoring the police band. They've run up the flag, but no one's spotted us yet, or guessed which way we're running."

Thone continued working the phone. If worse came to worst, he could always use the American agent and the girl as hostages to buy more time. His next call was to a person in military intelligence at Fort Benning who owed him something considerably more tangible than a mere soul. If Thone burned, Hackshaw knew he would, as well. The Fortress Arms CEO glanced at his watch. In minutes, De Moray would be at the office they'd set up in Miami. He decided to delay contacting the man until Goss arrived with the car.

The number he used for Hackshaw was a personal number, because the Army captain's nine-to-five shift was over with.

"Captain Hackshaw."

"Wiley," Thone said, "I just killed two military intelligence agents at my country club. You could say I'm not having a good day."

"God Almighty! And you're calling me at home?"

"We needed to talk. I assumed that you'd be there."

"Is this line secure?"

"No. And they might be tracing this call." Thone was lying. Until today, the phone line had never been used and there was no reason it would ever be tied to him.

"Shit."

"If you hang up," Thone said authoritatively, "I'll hang you out to dry whether they get their hands on me or not. You might not yet be compromised, but I am. I need to know how deeply this investigation runs."

"Damn, I don't know. This is the first I've heard of it."

Thone put edged steel into his voice. "The last thing that I want to hear right now is that the man I bought and paid for to snitch off military intelligence about my business hasn't a clue to what's going on."

"This has got to be something new."

"Get a handle on it and get back to me."

"Yes, sir."

Thone hung up and dropped the phone into the gym bag. Through the Plexiglas bubble of the helicopter's nose, he saw the tan sands of Topanga State Beach and the crystal blue of Santa Monica Bay lapping at the fringes. Vacationers and sunbathers littered the beach.

The helicopter began its descent. Sandison handled the whirlybird expertly. The spinning rotors played hell with the beach scene. Whipping sand sprayed over a nearby cluster of volleyball players and sent them scurrying for cover. The gale force of the wind shoved a red plastic ice chest from a small family's folding picnic table and corkscrewed the red-and-white-checked tablecloth after it.

The skids touched down onto the loose surface as three nearby sand castles were beaten back into the beach. Thone was in motion almost at once, dropping from the seat and scanning for Goss and the Cadillac Seville. Instead, his eyes locked on the bronze star pinned to the chest of the mustached man striding toward him.

"Los Angeles County Sheriff's Office. You people hold it right there." The man smoothly drew a Colt .45 Government Model from his hip holster and squared it up in a two-handed Weaver stance as he continued to advance.

Thone covertly glanced at Sandison as he came to a halt. Sand trickled into his shoes. At his side, no more than ten feet away, the pilot shook his head.

The sheriff's deputy stopped. "If your partner does go for it, I'm still going to drop you first." The pistol never wavered.

Reluctantly Thone raised his hands above his head.

Then the flat crack of a heavy-calibered rifle rang out across the beach. The deputy's head blew apart and started a fresh chorus of screams from the beach crowd. Three lifeguards, two male and one female, who'd been racing toward the scene abruptly stopped in their tracks. A second bullet whacked into the sand at their feet, scattering them into fearful dives.

Gazing farther up the beach, Thone saw Goss calmly leaning across the open door of the maroon Cadillac, a Mini-14 Ranch Rifle in hand. The munitions king drew his own pistol and started an unconcerned jog for the luxury car. Sandison was at his heels.

As Thone clambered into the back seat of the Cadillac, Goss fired four more rounds to keep the beach-goers in their place.

The air-conditioning was welcome relief as Thone belted himself in. Sandison was beside him, rolling down the window and thrusting the muzzle of the mini-Uzi through the opening. Tossing the rifle into the passenger seat beside him, Goss slid behind the wheel and shoved the transmission into gear. The luxury car purred out of the parking area toward the Pacific Coast Highway.

"The plates?" Thone asked.

"Spare set in the trunk." Goss met his employer's gaze in the rearview mirror. "I'll have them changed as soon as we make a calm harbor."

Thone nodded and unflexed the flip phone. He wasn't sure who had tumbled to him. Military intelligence had been a surprise. He'd known about the covert agency dogging his heels and almost had a lead on them. He punched in the Miami office number for De Moray.

He he raked his fingers through his hair. He might be on the run for the moment, but he wasn't without resources. Dozens of people who could become the Huntsman were scattered around the globe, just waiting to be unleashed. He knew the resulting carnage would provide more than enough of a smokescreen for him to make his escape.

His revenge would be a more exacting process. The thought made him smile an instant before De Moray came on the line. "Tell me you have a name, my friend."

"Harold Brognola," the Cajun answered confidently. "And more than that, I've got the son of a bitch in my sights even as we speak."

3

The passenger carrier Mack Bolan clung to was sandwiched between the coal car and burning wreckage of the other passenger coach. The impact drove it from the rails.

His grip was torn loose instantly. The passenger carrier listed to the right, balanced precariously for a moment, then started the plunge toward the ground. The warrior shoved free of the train car and leaped clear. His boots hit the ground hard and the shock ran up his legs. Rolling to the side, the Executioner fisted the Ithaca as he brought it up.

Bloody Wind terrorists had spilled from the coal car in controlled falls that took them behind rocks and bushes. Autofire ripped through the brush seeking the Stony Man warriors.

Adjusting the mike of the headset, Bolan tapped the transmit button. "Phoenix One."

"Go." Katz sounded agitated. "Are you okay?"

"So far." Bolan pointed the shotgun at a terrorist who'd pushed himself to a standing position. He pulled the trigger, and the spread of 12-gauge buckshot took the man in the upper body. The corpse fell backward.

"We'll be right there." A burst of autofire carried over the transmission, then was cut off as Katz dropped out of the loop.

A handful of 7.62 mm rounds chopped into the olive tree the Executioner had been using for cover. White splinters jumped out under the moonlight and flew toward his face. He returned fire, picking off the shooter and sending the man spinning out into the open. He thumbed fresh shells into the Ithaca.

Scanning the toppled train car, Bolan saw McCarter scrambling free of the wreckage. Bullets scarred the sides of the passenger carrier as the terrorists tracked the Briton. An instant later, Calvin James appeared at the rear of the car, backlit by twisting flames. The ex-SEAL maintained a grip on the young woman's arm, hurrying her forward.

Sally Coleman stumbled, then sprawled on the ground. James didn't hesitate about taking up a defensive position in front of the woman. In his hands, the Uzi inscribed a death circle that cut into the ranks of the closing terrorists.

Abandoning his position, Bolan plucked two antipersonnel grenades from his combat harness, yanked the pins, slipped the spoons, then tossed the bombs toward the coal car. The explosives sailed true. Twin explosions sounded a heartbeat later, dealing out death and injury in a twenty-five-foot radius.

By that time the warrior was at James's side. Bolan reached down and took the woman's arm, helping her to her feet and holding her close as he broke for cover. James and McCarter provided defensive fire.

Without warning, three Bloody Wind terrorists came at them from behind the wreckage. They lowered their weapons into position. Before they could fire, the Land Rover carrying Manning and Katz slewed around the wrecked train cars. The terrorists turned to face the new threat.

Manning didn't give them a chance to set themselves. The Land Rover's engine snarled as the big Canadian floored the accelerator. Tufts of grass and rock were torn loose by the four-wheel drive. Bounding over the rough terrain, the Land Rover smashed into the three terrorists and scattered them.

Standing on the running board, a MAC-10 clenched in his only fist, his right arm and wicked hook of curved metal holding on to the door frame behind him, Katz fired controlled bursts into targets he found.

Bolan changed directions at once, almost picking the woman up now as he sprinted for the Land Rover that Manning had brought to a rocking stop. Letting the MAC-10 hang from the strap around his neck, Katz stepped down from the running board and opened the door.

"I've got her," the Israeli said, helping the woman into the cab.

Bolan vaulted onto the vehicle's rooftop after sheathing the Ithaca in the calf holster. The ARES TARG heavy machine gun they'd brought with them had been bolted into position on top of the Land Rover by Manning and Katz. Chambered in 12.7 mm ammunition that came in hardball, armor-piercing and incendiary rounds, the TARG was a deadly piece of equipment. Bolan touched off bursts as McCarter and James ran for the 4X4.

Cylindrical in shape, the spent casings were dumped out the end of the barrel rather than a port. The four-barreled revolving cylinder picked up fresh rounds from the ammunition box through a feed rotor. The backlash from the recoil was terrific.

The Executioner focused on the targets, becoming a merciless gun sight as he tracked down the terrorists. The wave advancing on the Land Rover broke and dissipated.

Return fire became sporadic and wild, most of the rounds never coming close to the vehicle.

Standing on the running board, Katz pounded the MAC-10's gun butt against the rooftop. "Go, Gary."

Manning let out the clutch and the Land Rover vaulted forward. Hanging on to the luggage racks so he wouldn't put any more strain on the temporary braces holding the TARG, Bolan watched as the terrorists attempted to gather a pursuit force. Before they got under way, James lowered the tailgate and fired into their midst. McCarter and Katz added to the firepower an instant later, cutting down their attackers' enthusiasm.

Taking advantage of the brief respite, Bolan unhooked the ammunition box from the TARG and glanced into it. He estimated he had less than thirty rounds left. The Land Rover bounced over the railway tracks when Manning cut behind the burning train cars, the heat of the flames washing over the Executioner as he unstrapped the reserve ammunition box.

The headset crackled for attention, then Kurtzman's voice joined them in the com loop. "Stony teams, this is Stony Base."

"Go, Base," Bolan responded. The reserve ammunition box clicked into place. He checked the feed rotor and made sure the action was clear.

"You've got three bogies bearing down on your position. You should have visual sighting of them at any time."

"Affirmative, Stony Base." Bolan peered into the darkness shrouding the uneven countryside. "G-Force, are you in the loop?"

"Roger," Grimaldi radioed back. "I'm racked and stacked, buddy. You guys make the exfiltration point, I'm your ticket out of here."

"I'm going to hold you to that."

McCarter's voice rang out clear and sharp. "I've spotted our bloody bogies, mates. Eleven o'clock and coming on strong."

Shifting his attention, Bolan glanced ahead of them. Three military jeeps were bearing down on them from two hundred yards out, coming hard, trailing clouds of gray dust behind them. At least two of the vehicles had mounted machine guns, because the gunners cut loose. Two of the rounds knocked sparks from the Land Rover's nose and smashed a headlight, cutting down their visibility.

"Oh, shit," Manning growled.

Before his comment could fade out on the headset frequency, the Land Rover hit a large, flat boulder. Almost instantly they were airborne. The engine whined with effort. Like an ungainly duck, the Land Rover returned to the earth, rocking hard from side to side.

Bolan maintained his grip with difficulty as Manning downshifted and brought the vehicle back under control. The jeeps, coming from the other direction, had rapidly closed the distance to a 150 yards.

"David," the Executioner said, "there's an M-249 in one of those equipment cases."

"Got it, mate. I get loaded up here, those Bloody Wind bastards are going to know it, too."

"Gary, we're not exactly running on stealth mode here," Bolan said. "Hit those fog lights so you can see what's ahead of us and let's move."

"Right." The fog lights mounted on the front of the Land Rover flared to life and burned away the night. With the destructive energy behind the 12.7 mm rounds in the TARG, he didn't have to worry about being precise. Locking on to the jeep's headlights would provide enough of a target. And the loads in the second ammunition box were primarily incendiary, with every third one being a tracer.

The Executioner shifted around on the luggage rack and squared himself behind the machine gun. The familiar *whump* of the M-249 thudded into the circus of sounds spinning around them. Bolan registered the grenade launcher's impact against a tree only a few yards in front of the lead jeep. The 40 mm warhead struck fire from the tree and split it in two.

"Bloody hell," McCarter stated calmly.

Bolan aimed by instinct. There was no way for a set shot from the top of the Land Rover. The jeeps were less than eighty yards away. Squeezing off five- and six-round bursts, the Executioner tracked his prey. When the third burst slammed into the grillwork fronting the lead jeep and struck sparks, he fired a sustained barrage that stitched the entire vehicle.

The incendiary rounds punched through the engine and set it on fire. Evidently the gasoline feed lines caught as well, because the driver was unable to stop the jeep before it became a rolling pyre. Flaming figures leaped from the vehicle's rear and looked like fiery ghosts scrambling through the trees and brush.

The M-249 coughed again. This time the grenade was more on target, erupting under the driver's side and flipping the jeep over to land upside down.

The surviving jeep slowed and kept its distance, falling into line along their backtrail.

Scrambling for position, Bolan crawled around to the front of the Land Rover and rotated the TARG. His legs stuck out over the windshield as he brought the final target into view.

Manning had found a relatively level part of terrain that turned out to be some sort of trail. Katz and Bolan had uncovered it during their earlier survey of the satellite recon pictures of the area. They were less than a minute from the exfiltration point.

"Striker," Kurtzman cut in.

"Go." Bolan brought the TARG to his shoulder smoothly.

"They just got a chopper into the air at the hardsite. It'll be there in minutes. And they've mounted more cavalry."

"Roger, Stony Base." Bolan concentrated on the jeep. They'd known they were cutting the operation close just taking the ground troops into consideration. There'd been no Intel about the helicopter. He squeezed the trigger, and green tracers thudded into the ground just to the left of the jeep.

The Bloody Wind driver pulled hard in the other direction, almost overcompensating. The jeep hit rough terrain and bounded upward for an instant.

Taking the opportunity afforded him, Bolan squeezed the TARG's trigger and raked autofire along the jeep's chassis. Flames engulfed the front end of the vehicle and crawled up over the fender wells as it thumped back against the ground. The Executioner fired again and took out both front tires, listening to the TARG cycle empty.

The jeep spun crazily and skidded off the trail to smash against a copse of trees.

"There's the chopper," Katz roared above the Land Rover's engine.

Bolan glanced into the sky and saw the winking landing lights of the small helicopter streaking toward them. He tapped the headset's transmitter button. "Phoenix Four."

"Go." Rafael Encizo sounded intent and ready.

"The aerial target?"

"I'm on it, but I don't know how much damage I can do with this M-60."

"Find out when it gets within range."

Manning roared up the last of the incline and braked, sending a scatter of loose rock over the nearby trees and bushes.

Bolan finished reattaching the nearly empty ammunition box to the TARG, then slipped the quick-release bolts on the tripod. Cradling the big gun in his arms, he dropped over the Land Rover's side. The familiar moan of the M-60 blasted into the night, covering the noises the team made as they debarked from the 4X4.

Manning helped James with Sally Coleman, hustling her toward the waiting fiberglass-and-steel platform they were using for their escape. Two telescoping PVC poles had been placed in the ground on either side of the platform about ten feet out. Stretching upward roughly twenty feet, they held a heavy cable in Ys at their ends. The platform was eight feet square with side walls of eighteen inches, barely enough room for the six people who would be riding inside.

"Yakov," Bolan said, "get Jack in here and let's get our team out."

The Israeli nodded and moved off toward the platform to make arrangements.

Sprinting over to where Encizo was dug in behind a shelter of fallen trees, Bolan focused on the helicopter flying toward their position. He listened to the rattle of communication between Katz and Grimaldi and knew the ace pilot was winging his way toward them. A glance over his shoulder showed him that Manning, McCarter and James were breaking out the packs of foam cushions and using them to pad the unforgiving hard surface of the platform. The four strands of cable linking the platform to the cable suspended from the telescoped rods were almost invisible.

Purple tracers blasted from Encizo's M-60. Brass spilled out from the light machine gun, and the tracers made an uneven whip that tongued out for the small helicopter.

Suddenly a wave of 20 mm cannonfire rocked their position. The impacts ripped bark from the fallen trees and chopped through branches and leaves.

"They're armed," Encizo stated unnecessarily.

Bolan settled the TARG onto the thick oak and waited. The thirty rounds would be effective against the helicopter, but he'd have to wait until the time was right.

"The rest of the vultures aren't wasting time, either," the Cuban said, pointing.

Following the direction the Phoenix warrior indicated, Bolan saw a line of vehicles speeding toward their position. They'd be overrun once the land troops arrived because they lacked the firepower to hold their ground. And there was no rescue force waiting in the wings. He tapped the transmit button on the headset. "G-Force."

"On your go," the pilot responded.

"Striker," Katz said, "when we pop the flares for the pickup, we're going to become an immediate target."

"We're a target anyway," Bolan replied. "At least with G-Force, we're a moving one."

"Agreed. But we can set up smoke canisters around the perimeters and hopefully stave off some of the assault."

"That's a good idea. Get it done." Bolan took smoke grenades from his own combat gear. Slipping into the night, with the chattering bursts of Encizo's M-60 hammering in his ears, the warrior swept the outer perimeter at a run. He armed the smoke grenades and tossed them carefully. Multicolored clouds of smoke rose up at once. The wind was calm on this side of the mountain, allowing the smoke to pool into gaseous walls.

The ground troops were firing blind now, barely within range of the mounted machine guns. Only the helicopter had a clear field of fire.

Noting the buzz of the cargo plane's engine overhead, Bolan looked up in time to see Grimaldi heeling down out of the sky. "G-Force."

"Clean and green, pal." The cargo plane started descending in a lazy spiral.

Abruptly the helicopter broke off the attack on the mountaintop and gained altitude as it headed to confront the cargo plane.

"You've got a hawk on your tail, mate," McCarter radioed.

"Affirmative," Grimaldi said. "I picked him up. Son of a bitch isn't shy at all." The cargo plane rolled over and zoomed toward the chopper. "Bet he thinks I came to the picnic with nothing but purity of heart." When the cargo plane came out of the roll, the twin .50-caliber machine guns mounted under the wings came to life. Green tracers raced toward the helicopter, missing by inches and causing the pilot to dive for cover.

Bolan knew the weapons onboard the cargo plane hadn't been keyed into an arms computer and Grimaldi was shooting from the hip. He glanced through the hanging smoke and saw the lights of the approaching vehicles. "Katz!" he yelled above the din.

"Yes."

"Load up. We're running out of time." Bolan tapped the headset transmit button. "G-Force, break it off and make the lift."

"Roger, Striker." The cargo plane veered from an attack dive and swirled around to lose even more altitude. It came from the southwest, flying only a few dozen feet above the ground. A moment later Katz and his team popped the emergency flares and lighted up the site in penetrating crimson.

Bolan tapped Encizo on the shoulder. "Go."

The Cuban eyed him. "What about you?"

"I've got to try for the chopper. If it stays airborne, we're all dead."

Encizo gathered the M-60 in his arms and glanced toward the sky. "You don't have much time. You miss the pickup, you're on your own."

"Maybe I'll be lucky."

"I hope so, amigo, because Katz will have my ass if you don't make it." Encizo slapped him on the shoulder, then turned and ran for the platform.

Bolan hunkered behind the TARG and lifted it. Looking back at the platform, he saw that Katz had gotten everyone loaded and braced for the pickup. The plane was less than a thousand yards out now, sailing smoothly. He couldn't see the dangling hook attached to the winch line, but he knew it was there.

Above, the helicopter had come about and took up an interception course. Somewhere on the other side of the smoke walls, the sound of the straining jeep engines grated into the maelstrom of noise.

Bolan snugged the TARG's stock into his cheek and leaned the barrel against the fork of a tree. The chopper came across the sighting blade of the heavy machine gun. Moving slightly, the Executioner made the adjustment to lead the aircraft, then squeezed the trigger, firing through the remaining ammo.

Less than 150 yards up, the tracers dug into the sheet metal sides and Plexiglas nose of the chopper. In seconds, the incendiary rounds ripped the aircraft to pieces, leaving only a whirling orange and black fireball and falling, flaming shrapnel in their wake.

Abandoning the empty TARG where it lay, Bolan gathered his feet under him and sprinted for the platform. Even as fragments of the helicopter rained around him, the first of the terrorist vehicles roared through the curtain of smoke.

If he'd been at the proper altitude, Bolan knew he'd have been on a collision course with the cargo plane. The platform was in front of him and the Bloody Wind was at his heels. Muzzle-flashes from Phoenix Force's guns danced along the platform. He put his feet down hard, trying to take advantage of the covering fire.

Then, all at once, he knew he wasn't going to make it. Grimaldi was going to reach the cable with the hook before he could reach the platform. Perspiration streamed down his body, sticking the blacksuit to him as his mind raced. A bullet thrummed by his ear. Knowing it was his last-ditch hope, he yanked the collapsible grappling hook and knotted line from its place on his combat harness. The hooks finned out when he pressed the release button. He threaded the free end of the line through his combat harness.

The warrior was forty feet from the platform when the winch hook made contact with the cable between the telescoped poles. Sparks flew as metal rubbed on metal, then the poles spun away and the platform lifted from the ground. Grimaldi handled the winch line perfectly, paying out the line so the sudden start didn't snap the cable. The passengers were still buffeted by the immediate momentum.

Bolan was aware of the jeep closing on him when he made his cast with the grappling hook. His arm muscles burned with the effort. For a moment he thought he'd missed and was preparing to dive for cover and come up firing. Then the hook dropped over the edge of the platform. Almost immediately, the line snapped taut.

Not braced for the sudden pull, Bolan was swept off his feet and yanked upward. The sudden constriction of the combat harness around his chest crushed the wind from his lungs. He maintained his hold on the line and didn't let it slip back through the harness.

By the time he regained his breath, he was well above tree toplevel.

"Striker," Manning called out from above.

Still spinning slightly because of the slipstream of wind, Bolan had difficulty spotting the barrel-chested Canadian. "Here."

"Good enough. You hang on down there for just a minute, and we'll save you the trouble of climbing up."

"Thanks." Bolan recovered his balance and managed a vertical position. He peered through the darkness below. To the south, the train was still burning, and the countryside was littered with jeep and helicopter wreckage. A few muzzle-flashes sprinkled the ground near the exfiltration point, but they were already well out of range. As Manning pulled him up to the platform, the Executioner's mind was already turning to the other facets of the operation. Now that the Stony Man teams had uncovered Hayden Thone and the threat Fortress Arms posed, they still had to figure out everything that was at stake. Then put a stop to the man.

4

Miami, Florida

Alexander De Moray slipped the maître d' a fifty-dollar bill with the skill of a street dip from New York City.

The maître d' inclined his head slightly and gave an ingratiating smile. There was even a slight warmth in his bloodshot gray eyes. "Of course we can get you that table, sir. And you're right, the lady does deserve the very best." He snapped his fingers at a pair of busboys, then pointed to the littered booth in a corner of the restaurant.

Standing at six-three and carrying two hundred pounds of lean, corded muscles primarily in his chest and arms, De Moray knew he had the attention of several women in the Blue Duck restaurant. Even the more jaded female citizens of Miami appeared interested in turning for another look.

His hair was a thick shock of inky black and hung down in a loose tangle over his forehead. His hard-planed face spoke volumes about a life filled with violence and earnest intent. The dark charcoal jacket was expensive and tastefully tailored, setting off the maroon turtleneck underneath when combined with the dark slacks.

"Is he here?" his companion asked.

He looked at her as if she'd made a charming comment about the weather. He didn't know her real name, and it didn't matter. For some reason, he could almost remember kissing her but he couldn't remember the circumstances or when. Two days ago, she'd thought she was a disk jockey at a radio station in Memphis. Now she thought she was the Huntsman, a trained assassin who could live forever.

"Yes," De Moray replied, "but you need to relax before you give yourself away. Brognola isn't some wet-nosed pup fresh from a police academy. If you're going to take him out, you're going to have to show more finesse."

"Where?" She was tall and auburn haired. Her green eyes glittered with intensity. Tanned and fit, she looked sleek in the peach print wrap that showed off her cleavage and long legs. Her white handbag looked small, but he knew from experience that it was big enough to hold a 10 mm S&W Model 1006.

"Wait."

The maître d' returned. "This way, please."

De Moray held out his arm. After a moment, the woman looped hers through his. He led her to the table, knowing there were a number of people who watched them. He also knew it didn't matter. None of the people they were stalking knew him or the woman, and they wouldn't see them again until it was too late. After they were seated, De Moray ordered for both of them.

"Can I see him from here?" the woman asked.

De Moray took out a pack of cigarettes and lighted one, carefully keeping from her view, between his cupped palms, the Vietnamese beer lid on the Zippo. Seeing the bottle cap would only confuse her. He knew she had one on her key case because she'd shown it to him that morning. After all the years of seeing them in the hands of others who were convinced they were him, it was still unsettling. "Yes. At two o'clock behind you."

She took a compact out of her purse and acted as if she were checking her makeup.

It still amazed De Moray how easily the altered personalities accepted the sex changes between vessels. Despite being briefed on the whole process by Thone and the psychosquads he'd employed, the Cajun realized he'd rather just accept things as they were than understand them.

"I see him."

De Moray let out a lungful of air, leaning back as their waiter poured out glasses of champagne. He studied their quarry himself. It wasn't the first time he'd seen Harold Brognola up close, but he was aware as a professional predator that something could always be learned of the prey.

"So when do I kill him?" The woman's voice was flat and without emotion.

"When I say so," De Moray replied, "and not a moment before." He watched the table all the way across the large dining room without appearing to do so.

Brognola was a big man with large hands. De Moray knew from the dossier that had been assembled on him that the big Fed was head of a sensitive operations group within the Justice Department. The investigators Thone used had built a case for Brognola being the guiding hand behind the covert force chewing holes in the illegal-arms business Fortress Arms was secretly conducting. There were at least three teams across the globe, apparently operating with tacit sanction that wouldn't surface to the public eye.

Brognola himself had been assigned—grudgingly, Thone's investigators had discovered—to the multinational crime task force digging into the counterfeit currency flooding a number of countries. Fortress Arms was behind that, as well, and some of the illegal-arms shipments the covert teams had taken down would have proof of that. The noose was growing tighter around the Fortress Arms operation, but it was also exposing Brognola's involvement.

Judging from the reactions at the table across the room, Brognola was having problems of his own. His chief point of contention appeared to be George Cosgrove, the Miami-based Treasury agent. According to the Intel De Moray had received after returning from his jaunt in Europe, trying to track down the agent designated Striker, the crime task force should have been headed up through the Treasury Department, not the Department of Justice. A lot of political toes had been stepped on to make Brognola the chief chair of the group.

And that had been the first indication that Brognola was more than what he'd seemed.

The food arrived, and De Moray watched the woman eat. She seemed to derive no pleasure from the act, turning it into a purely mechanical action. He, on the other hand, enjoyed the meal and took his time with it. Too many times when he'd been young and hungry growing up, he'd watched tourists getting pampered in his native New Orleans. The Army Special Forces, followed by the CIA, then Hayden Thone, had all upscaled his life. He spent his days in luxury now, and he didn't intend to see that change.

Brognola was a threat, so the Fed had to go. But watching the man at the other table as the Treasury agent became visibly recalcitrant, De Moray began exploring the other possibilities. He wished he could overhear the conversation at the other table.

HAL BROGNOLA MET George Cosgrove's accusing stare without flinching. The meal was beginning to take on aspects of the Last Supper.

"This Judas sold us out," the Treasury agent said again. Cosgrove was a big, solid man. Ex-military, he still wore his iron-gray hair in a close crop. Crow's-feet at his eyes emphasized the dark bags under them.

Brognola figured a rubber hose and a naked light bulb glaring in his face would have suited the situation. Buying time and showing he wasn't about to be pushed, the head Fed reached into his pocket and pulled out a cigar. After biting off the end, he tucked the cigar in a corner of his mouth without lighting it and prepared to open the bidding.

"I didn't sell anybody out," he said coldly.

"The hell you didn't," Cosgrove exploded.

Michael Ferris, Cosgrove's partner, leaned forward. "Hey, buddy, let's take a chill pill here." He was twenty years younger than the other Treasury agent. "Give the guy a chance to explain."

Cosgrove pinned Brognola with his gaze. "That what you want? A chance to explain?"

The big fed silently stood his ground. He hadn't wanted the assignment to begin with, but had given in to pressure from the White House. Cosgrove had evidently tapped some of his Intel relays and recovered information he'd sent to Stony Man Farm. Although the Treasury agent hadn't been able to find out who the receiving station was, he had known that Brognola was relaying information. The pages in the manila envelope at Cosgrove's elbow were damning. Working inside the international task force investigating the flood of funny money, he'd diverted information that might normally have reached the group. It was important to give the Stony Man teams a chance to crack the paper trail without outside intervention from a dozen different governments that might slow down the hunt.

"No," Brognola said quietly.

"No?" Cosgrove seemed incredulous.

"Mr. Brognola," Harry Wu, the Hong Kong representative said, "the charges leveled against you are very serious ones. If true, you've broken faith with us."

The big Fed faced the other international cop. "I know that."

"And your answer?" That was from Pierre Napier, the French agent.

"Wouldn't satisfy any of you." Brognola tried to relax in his chair but couldn't. Lunch at the Blue Duck had been arranged by Lyle Kirkus, one of the task force members from the Dade County Sheriff's Office. At first he'd thought it was just a distraction from the work load. They'd racked up some busts around Miami since starting up, and had fed information to other law-enforcement agencies around the world. The task force had been responsible for a number of successes against the counterfeiting rings globally.

But he'd slowed down the information flow, and Cosgrove was aware of it.

"Whose pocket are you in?" Cosgrove demanded.

Brognola took the insult stoically. Inside, his stomach churned but he resisted the impulse to reach for the roll of antacid tablets he always carried.

"How much did it take for you to sell this operation out?" Cosgrove asked, pushing himself to his feet.

Across the table, Brognola stood as well and took the cigar from his mouth. "I didn't sell out anyone. We made clean busts, took down a lot of weapons and phony cash.

If I was in somebody's pocket, that shit wouldn't have went down."

"You're a snitch," Cosgrove accused, his face purpling with rage. He stabbed his finger at Brognola. "You ratted us out to somebody, and I want to know who."

"Back off," Brognola said in a voice tight with control. "I've been fighting for this country for decades, and I won't stop till I've drawn my last breath. My record speaks for itself."

"Impugning your character isn't what we're here for," Harry Wu said tacitly.

"Maybe it's not your intent," the head Fed growled, locking eyes with Cosgrove, "but it's certainly his."

"We just want to know who these people are that you've been in contact with," Wu continued.

Brognola waited a beat. There was no way he could talk about the Stony Man Farm hardsite even if he was inclined to. The only reason it worked as well as it did was because of its secrecy. "I'm not at liberty to say."

The other task force members took a collective breath and stared at him.

The big Fed dropped his napkin in his empty plate and pulled enough money to cover the dinner and the tip from the wallet inside his jacket. He tucked the bills under his water glass as he stood. "Gentlemen, the way I see it, you've got a lot to talk about while I'm gone. So why don't you get to it and let me know. You all know the number of my hotel room." He squared his shoulders and left the table.

Instead of heading out to the parking lot and his rental car, he headed to the back of the restaurant where phones were mounted on a polished wood wall opposite the bathroom doors. His lunch rolled queasily in his stomach. While he crunched antacid tablets, he used his calling card and placed a call to the White House. A moment later he was informed that the President wasn't available due to a conference call with some heads of state in the Middle East.

Using the calling card again, he placed a call to one of the many cutout numbers he had for the Farm. The back of his neck prickled, and he knew someone was watching him. While the cutout kicked the call through various switchboards, he glanced back into the dining room.

For a moment he locked eyes with a redhead who gave him a small smile. Beyond her, he saw Cosgrove watching him intently. He broke the eye contact slowly, then focused on the phone.

Barbara Price answered on the second ring.

Brognola identified himself. "It's nice to hear a friendly voice," he told the mission controller.

"How bad is it?" she asked without preamble.

"I've been blown here. A Treasury agent named Cosgrove has tumbled to some of the communiqués between me and the Farm."

"How?"

"I'm not sure."

"The Farm's integrity?"

"As far as I know, we're intact there. But I have a feeling I'm not going to be in a position to do anything from this end much longer."

"I don't know that you could do much there anyway," Price said. "Hayden Thone gunned down two military intelligence officers at his country club less than ten minutes ago. The man's on the run."

"Where?"

"I don't know." Price sounded tired. In the background there was the noise of computer keys clacking. "Aaron and his team have assembled a lot of information on Thone, De Moray and Fortress Arms, but most of it is incongruent as yet. When we find the picture, we'll be in a position to take our best guess."

"Man's got to have a rabbit hole somewhere."

"We'll find it."

"I know." Brognola was certain she and the Stony Man teams would. It wouldn't be the first miracle they'd accomplished. "How did military intelligence get involved?"

"They found some of the same records we were looking at. The bust Able made in Sitka leaked Intel back through the RCMP offices. They fielded a team after Thone before I could get Able into the area."

Brognola knew Thone's plans—whatever they were— were starting to unravel. A number of countries were already working on the illegal-arms shipments, as well, including the United States. It was only a matter of time until more hounds took up the chase, muddying even more the trail they were following. "I'm going to give the Man a call, see if I can shake loose from here and do something more productive. How'd things go in Italy?"

"Everybody's safe. I'm supposed to have a telecommunications link with Striker and Phoenix in twenty minutes. Able Team has a fistful of federal warrants and is about to invade Clay Pigeons."

"The Fortress Arms shooting gallery out in L.A.?"

"Yes."

"Thone won't be there."

"No, but it might give us another rung in the ladder."

"Let me know how it goes."

"Right."

Brognola cradled the receiver and tried the White House once more. The President still couldn't take his call. Hanging up, he went to the bathroom to wash his hands

and face, feeling a need to get clean after the verbal war at
the table. He'd known going in that he would probably end
up in an untenable position playing a double agent for the
task force. There was no way to explain that he hadn't betrayed them without giving up the Farm.

He rinsed his face and hands in the sink, ignoring the tall
guy with the curly black hair who walked in after him.
When he blotted his face dry on paper towels, he looked up
in the mirror and saw Cosgrove standing behind him.

"How much did you get paid for *that* phone call?" the
Treasury agent demanded.

Brognola chose to ignore the man, knowing there was no
right thing he could do.

"Whoever it was," Cosgrove said, "they've got to have
awfully deep pockets to buy a hot dog like you. I've seen
your records. You were a good cop once."

"I still am." Brognola glanced at the door. Cosgrove
was standing between him and the exit. "You want to
move?"

"Going to pick up your money?"

The dark-haired man was watching from the open stall
three doors down. A look of sardonic amusement mixed
with expectation twisted his lips.

"You're out of line," Brognola said.

"Not from where I see it."

Choosing discretion as the better part of valor for the
moment, the big Fed tried to step around the Treasury
agent. Before he got halfway, Cosgrove dropped a heavy
hand on his shoulder and pulled to spin him, intending to
catch him across the upper chest with a forearm shiver.

Brognola slapped the blow away with his open hand,
then stepped inside Cosgrove's arms before the man could
react. His free hand drifted over the Treasury agent's fu-
tile attempt at another blow, then clamped tight around the

guy's throat. Using his body weight, Brognola shoved Cosgrove hard enough against the wall to drive the wind from the man's lungs.

Cosgrove attempted to knee him in the groin, but Brognola turned away and held the Treasury agent pinned against the wall. Swinging wildly, Cosgrove managed to hit Brognola on the shoulder, but the blow lacked any strength. The big Fed reached up and slapped the Treasury agent's forehead hard enough to bounce his skull off the wall.

"Don't," Brognola growled in warning. "Professional courtesy ended some time ago. You want to take this to the sandlot level, I'll kick your ass up between your shoulder blades. You read me?"

Cosgrove's face turned beet-red, but he didn't make a reply.

"Hal."

Brognola gradually became aware that the bathroom door was open and a crowd had gathered. He kept his eyes locked on Cosgrove.

Ferris spoke again, his voice calm. "Let go of my partner and step back. There's no need to air all our dirty laundry for everyone to see."

"You through with this?" Brognola asked Cosgrove.

"For now. But there'll be another time."

Releasing the Treasury agent, Brognola stepped back and made his way through the crowd of international law-enforcement officers. He breathed out through his mouth forcefully to get his emotions under control, letting his breath come back on its own through his nose. For a moment he looked into the redhead's gaze as he passed her table. The warm smile on her lips never touched her eyes.

He passed through the main entrance under the watchful eye of the maître d', then stepped into the gathering gloom settling over Miami. Thoughts of Cosgrove were pushed out of his mind by the greater danger Hayden Thone represented while loose. The arms industrialist had some very serious ties to terrorist groups thought to be separate entities. The attack in Jerusalem that Phoenix Force had only succeeded in partially deflecting still weighed heavily on his mind and on the political scene.

He glanced at the bloodred sun sinking behind the conglomeration of buildings that made up downtown Miami and wondered how many more sunsets would pass before Thone struck back. He was betting it wouldn't be many.

5

Los Angeles

"You people can't come in here."

"Department of Justice, pal," Carl Lyons said, stepping through the double glass doors of Clay Pigeons. He gave his ID a workout and backed the guy off, then unfurled the first of the federal warrants to search the premises. "This piece of paper says I can go any damn place I want to."

The security guard's uniform was cast in bronze and green and looked striking. Sergeant chevrons decorated the lapels of his collar, and the front of his ballcap was an advertisement for Fortress Arms. The name tag on his breast pocket said he was F. Belknap.

The anteroom to the shooting gallery proper had more than a dozen people going through the Banana Republic jackets, shooting goggles, earplugs, books on handguns as a hobby, and glass cases holding various pistols and rifles manufactured by Fortress Arms. The smell of gun oil and perfume was thick on the air. All of the potential buyers had stopped their browsing and were watching the black-jacketed group of Alcohol, Tobacco and Firearms people file into the building.

Price had decided to complement Able Team with the ATF people to downplay any undue attention to Lyons and other members of the team. Lieutenant Martin O'Reilly was going to be the chief contact person for any PR reports and media interaction. It also circumvented the need for direct involvement with the Santa Monica PD and the chance that Lyons might be recognized by any old comrades-in-arms from his days on the LAPD.

"You," Lyons barked at the two men standing behind the counter between the two doors leading back into the shooting gallery, "get your hands up and step away from the counter. *Now.*"

They looked at each other but didn't move, looking slightly lost under the rack of colorful sweatshirts advertising Clay Pigeons over a black target silhouette.

The big ex-cop wore a black ATF jacket over a Minnesota Vikings T-shirt. His Colt Government Model .45 was in shoulder rigging, while his Colt Python .357 rode his right hip. He carried a Remington Model 870 12-gauge shotgun in his right hand. With a quick movement, he racked the slide and pointed it over their heads.

"Clear the area," he said in a cold voice, "or I'll clear it for you."

"Do it," a feminine voice commanded.

The men left the counter with their hands in the air.

Looking over his shoulder, Lyons found the speaker. She was tall and supple. Her platinum-blond locks had been shaved in the back and on the sides, leaving a punkish mop atop her head that still looked excitably feminine. She was dressed in black leather pants that hugged every gliding curve, and a lacy black vest that revealed a startling amount of cleavage. Already tall, the spiked cowboy boots on her feet brought her nearly up to Lyons's eye level.

"Do you want to tell me what this is about?" Her violet eyes gleamed with the challenge in her words. She folded her arms across her breasts.

"No." Lyons started to walk by her, intending to go through the nearest door to the shooting gallery. Kurtzman and Price had faxed the interior blueprints of the building as best as they knew them, so he had a working map of the area.

She put a hand against his chest to hold him back. "Maybe you don't know who I am. I'm—"

"Vanessa Dearborn," Lyons interrupted. "I know who you are, lady. Now get the hell out of my way and let me do my job."

"I manage this shooting gallery," she said, falling into step with him. "Anything that goes on here, I know about."

"Yeah?" Lyons gazed at her in open speculation, but didn't break stride. "Then maybe you'd like to tell me where the illegal-arms shipments are being held, and where I can find Salvatore Mancuso."

She didn't appear shaken. "Mancuso's not here. And as far as illegal guns, I don't know what you're talking about."

The ATF officers flowed in Lyons's wake, rounding up the scattered security force. They entered the small café area complete with catering services, the cubicles where gun clubs could meet privately, and drifted through the stalls opening up to the range proper. No one appeared willing to put up a fight.

O'Reilly trotted up to Lyons, his CAR-15 cradled in his arms. "What do you want to do about the civilians? I got a couple movie stars back there who don't want to get involved in this thing. Harnke tells me the media's already got wind of this, and after Thone gunned down those military intelligence guys less than a half hour ago, they're already making a beeline here.''

"Get 'em processed," Lyons said. "Anybody you can identify as a civilian, get them out the back doors as soon as possible. Those tabloids are going to have a field day with this anyway."

"You got it." The ATF man dropped back and started issuing orders over his walkie-talkie.

"And me?" Dearborn asked.

"You stay." Lyons stopped in front of the private office Thone had inside the range. The door was locked. "You got a key for this?"

"You want to search me?"

"And violate your civil rights so you can possibly get some of this shit thrown out of court later, babe?" Lyons gave her a cold grin. "I don't think so." He lifted his foot, cocked his leg and drove his boot into the door beside the locking mechanism.

Wood splintered and the door flew open.

Lyons stepped forward, swinging the Remington 12-gauge to cover the room's interior. A big teak desk was against the far wall, holding computer equipment, a phone and a marble desk set. Behind the desk, the wall was covered with framed pictures of Thone with movie stars of both sexes, politicians from all over the world and key figures in the NRA. A wet bar, fully stocked, was in the corner along the front wall to the side of the one-way glass that looked out over the shooting range.

Stepping inside, Lyons flicked on the lights. He laid the shotgun on the desktop and started going through the office planner and calendar with practiced ease.

"Do you really think Mr. Thone would write down when his next big illegal-arms shipment was?" Dearborn asked sarcastically.

"Lady, you never know what clever masterminds like your boss would write down." Lyons flipped through the pages. "They're so clever they figure they could get away with anything. Murder's only the beginning." The ear-throat headset he wore buzzed for his attention. "Go."

"Ironman, we've got the back doors secured." The speaker was Rosario Blancanales. Called the Politician because of his skills at communications and diplomacy, Blancanales had seen action in Vietnam with the Executioner as part of the elite Special Forces group, Pen-Team Able. "O'Reilly has given his men instructions to cut the civilians loose."

"Yeah. That came from me. A lot of innocents could be hurt by the fallout of this thing. They don't deserve it."

"Roger. We're on our way in."

"Any resistance?"

"No, but I've got some lawyers already interested in seeing the warrants we've got."

"They'll get their turn." Lyons moved away from the desk and dropped the planner into a pouch he pulled from his jacket pocket.

"I think that's personal property," Dearborn said. "You don't have a right to it."

"When I find Thone, he can file a complaint and get it back." Lyons studied the pictures behind the desk, keeping an eye on the woman. He thumbed the transmit button on the headset. "Gadgets."

"Yo."

"I'm waiting."

"I'm working. Shit, everything in this damn building is powered. Damn schematic looks like somebody turned over a bowl of spaghetti on it."

"Get back to me as soon as you know something."

"Right." Hermann Schwarz, called Gadgets and Wizard because of his proficiency with things electrical and mechanical, had also served a tour with Mack Bolan in the jungle. When it came to surveillance and booby traps—especially when working with everyday items—Schwarz had no peer.

Taking the walkie-talkie from his hip, Lyons keyed it to life and continued his search of the office. After learning of Thone's double homicide and disappearance, neither he nor Price had expected to find the man at the shooting range, but they couldn't pass up the chance at attaining further information about the arms industrialist and his plans. "O'Reilly."

"Go."

"What about Mancuso's car?"

"It's not in the parking garage. The valet said he left not ten minutes before we got here."

"Terrific. See if you can negotiate an APB on the car through the Santa Monica PD and L.A. County Sheriff's Office. If you need clout to get it done, let me know."

"Check."

Lyons saw the hairline crack in the wall behind the desk and fished out his Bowie knife from his boot. Inserting the thick blade, he pried around until he found the lock. Taking a two-fisted grip on the knife, he twisted hard.

With a harsh, metallic ping, the lock mechanism shredded. He shoved his fingers behind the panel and pulled, breaking the rest of the catches. An arsenal of weapons was revealed as the hidden door slid away. A variety of handguns, rifles and knives hung on pegs that ran from floor to ceiling. There was even a SEAL crossbow with a quiver of bolts.

"Ironman." Schwarz entered the office with Blancanales at his heels. Dressed in an ATF jacket, a blue-and-white baseball shirt, jeans, joggers and a camou-colored ballcap, Gadgets looked like an outfielder who'd seen the last of his salad days. A Beretta 92-F hung in shoulder leather under the jacket, and a H&K MP-5 swung from a Whip-it sling. He held a box covered with dials and switches in his hands, following it like a well witcher.

Blancanales had aristocratic features beneath longish salt-and-pepper hair, and a thin mustache. Built stocky and broad, he still moved lightly and quickly on his feet. He carried his H&K MP-5 in one hand and stayed alert.

"Oh, yeah," Schwarz said as he came to a halt against the far wall. He switched off the device he was carrying and clipped it to his belt, then ran his hands over the thermostat controls. The cover popped off in his hands, and he peered at the wiring with evident interest as he pulled a small screwdriver from the tool pouch at his belt.

"Something?" Lyons asked.

"Checking the power outages and schematics was a good idea," Schwarz said. "Looks like there's a whole floor buried beneath this building somewhere."

"And the thermostat controls?"

"What was that magic word Ali Baba used to get into the cave of the forty thieves?"

"Alikazam."

"Hell, that's close enough." With a final twist of the screwdriver, Schwarz stepped back. Almost without a sound, a portion of the wall rolled away to reveal a darkened recess.

"Care to say anything?" Lyons asked Dearborn as he produced a pair of cuffs.

She gazed at him coolly. "I'll want my lawyer."

"Of course you will." Expertly Lyons cuffed her to a desk leg out of reach of the weapons on the wall. She gazed at him demurely.

Blancanales and Schwarz took up flanking positions at the doorway.

"I got point," Lyons said. "Notify O'Reilly and the others and let them know what we found." He took a roll of ordnance tape from his jacket pocket and quickly taped a flashlight to the Remington 870's barrel. For the moment he kept the light off.

Stepping into the passageway, he followed the winding descent. The stairwell twisted enough that the light issuing from the office above was lost almost immediately.

By habit, Lyons counted the steps. At thirty-two, he stepped off onto the floor. He heard the voices almost immediately, noting from the heavy accent that the speakers were Jamaican.

A half dozen cars were parked to the right, but the voices were coming from the left. Lyons ignored the cars and made for the voices. The blueprints had contained information about the underground parking garage. He found a door primarily by feel, roughly twenty feet farther on. It had been left ajar, and pale yellow light bled through the crack.

The deal on the other side of the door was going down by the light of hand torches. Three wooden crates sat in the middle of the large room. More than a dozen Rastafarians were talking to a man with a blue business suit and long hair. He appeared ill at ease.

One of the Rastafarians opened the nearest crate and pulled out an Ingram M-10 submachine gun that was filmed with oily sweat. Murmurs of appreciation ran through the crowd. Another Rastafarian slammed a suitcase on the small table beside the man in the suit, then opened the locks with a key that hung around his neck. When he pushed the lid back, neat stacks of currency in rubber bands were revealed.

The deal apparently conducted to everyone's satisfaction, the Rastafarians brought hand trucks over from a neat line at a wall and slipped them under the crates.

Lyons glanced around the room. It was nearly fifty feet across, providing plenty of room for people involved in tense situations revolving around money and guns. Adjustable track lighting set the mood or helped chase away any paranoia. The small table beside the man in the suit was the only piece of furniture. On the other side of the room were a set of double doors and two golf carts.

"We got the back covered," Blancanales whispered in Lyons's ear, "but I don't think that tunnel goes that way."

Lyons flicked through his mental map of the building, matching compass points. "It doesn't, unless it twists and turns like a son of a bitch."

The sound of gunfire suddenly echoed from somewhere above, sounding very distant but unmistakable. In the center of the room, the Rastafarians froze for just an instant, then started pulling guns.

O'Reilly called for Lyons by his cover name. "Just went to hell in a handcart up here, buddy. A couple of my boys confronted a handful of Jamaican guys coming through the door loaded for bear. They eased around the marked units that just rolled up out front."

"Take them down and hold them," Lyons ordered. "They're part of the group taking delivery here in the basement level."

Without warning, the Rastafarians shot down the man in the suit, then turned their guns on Able Team's position. Bullets chopped into the door and walls around it, driving the Stony Man warriors back to cover. The Rastafarians moved to pull the crates toward the other exit.

Lyons reached into his jacket pockets and found a grenade. "Pol."

"Yeah?"

"Think you can take out the lights?"

"When?"

Lyons pulled the grenade's pin. "Now."

With an economy of motion, Blancanales leaned around the door frame. The H&K subgun chattered enthusiastic bursts that hurried the Rastafarians along their way. The 9 mm rounds clawed the fluorescent tubes from the ceiling mounts and plunged the room into darkness. Only the scattered muzzle-flashes created any illumination.

"Thunderflash," Lyons informed his teammates. He slipped the spoon and underhanded the grenade into the room. A heartbeat later, the grenade exploded, scattering light and noise. *"Move!"* The ex-LAPD cop was in motion at once. He flicked on the flashlight mounted on the Remington 870. The white beam licked out like an arrow in flight and swept the room from left to right like a radar detector.

A Rastafarian came into view in the ellipse of light, a dark screaming face brandishing a large silver revolver.

Lyons squeezed the shotgun's trigger, and the spray of double-aught buckshot made the face go away. He leaped over the corpse to continue the pursuit. Another man stepped into his path, not really knowing the Able Team warrior was on him until the Remington's heavy barrel crashed into his jaw and put him down.

Two of the crates had been fitted to the pulling assemblies mounted on the golf carts. The drivers wasted no time in getting underway.

Lyons's hiking boots thudded into the floor as he pursued them. At first he drew close, then they pulled away as the second gear kicked in. Anger surging through him, he fired the Remington dry while on the run. The buckshot patterns chewed splinters from both crates, but there was no clear shot at the men aboard the carts. He dropped the shotgun and drew the Colt 45 Government Model as he continued to run. They might have the speed, but it remained to be seen whether they had the distance.

The passage was already starting to slant upward, but the carts showed no signs of slowing. Sixty yards ahead of them, doors opened up in the ceiling, revealing a mechanized lift that creaked as it lowered.

Lifting the Colt .45 in both hands before him, Lyons aimed at the right rear tire on the lead golf cart. The tires were pneumatic, not hard rubber. He fired the clip dry, and sparks jumped from the concrete floor. But one of the rounds ripped into the tire, deflating it instantly. The flat tire, combined with the heavy load it was pulling, caused the golf cart to go out of control.

When the driver overcontrolled, the cart smashed into the corridor wall, almost turning sideways. The guy in the passenger seat bailed out and brought up his Uzi. A line of 9 mm bullets etched a pattern in the floor.

Without breaking stride, knowing Schwarz and Blancanales had brought up the rear to cover him, Lyons drew the .357 and fired three rounds into the gunner's chest. The hollowpoints spun the man and draped him over the golf cart's nose.

The driver pulled his pistol as he vaulted from the seat. He managed two shots as he ran for the other cart before Lyons cut him down.

Return fire from the other cart drove the big Able Team warrior to cover behind the wooden crate. He shucked the empty magazine from the .45 and rammed a fresh one home, then used a speed-loader to fill the .357's cylinder. Glancing back, he saw that Schwarz and Blancancales were locked into holding positions. He tapped the transmit button to access the channel. "Ready?"

"You figure now is a good time?" Schwarz asked.

Lyons looked at the cart hurtling toward the descending elevator lift. "I figure any later, there's going to be no time at all."

"I've got a Thunderflash primed," Blancanales offered.

"Do it," Lyons said as he lifted his jacket to cover his face. Bullets continued to ping and deflect from the golf cart. *"Now!"*

"It's away," Blancanales reported. A heartbeat later the thunderous detonation of the SAS thunder-and-lightning spectacular roared through the tunnel.

Lyons was up at once, rounding the golf cart with both pistols before him. He leaped over a corpse and chose his first target as the man came about with a sawed-off shotgun in his hands. Firing both his pistols, Lyons knew he hit the man between the throat and forehead with both rounds, then increased his pace while the body tumbled from the cart.

The vehicle skidded sideways as the driver applied the brake. Men broke from the elevator lift, making the effort to get to the weapons crate. Autofire whipped over Lyons's head. He dodged right.

Abruptly the gunner staggered backward, smashed by a continuous stream of bullets on deliberate select fire. Lyons recognized the sharp cracks of Schwarz's CAR-15. He trained the .45 on a man trying to climb through the opening in the floor. Evidently the Rastafarians were giving up all hope of getting away with the munitions. He fired three rounds.

The .45ACP hollowpoints ripped into the man's thighs and buttocks. Wounded and in pain, the Rastafarian released his hold and fell onto three of his comrades who were scrambling for position. One of them unleashed an Uzi, full-throttle, at Lyons.

The rolling thunder of the shots from the Able Team leader's .357 Magnum sounded like one continuous explosion. The fallen Jamaicans jerked as the bullets drilled into them.

Still on the move, Lyons leathered the Python and shifted the Army Colt to his right hand. He leaped for the top of the golf cart, caught himself on his free hand and pushed himself up. Sliding across the smooth surface of the short roof, he reached for the edge of the opening. The clank, hiss and ratcheting of gears signaled the lift's ascent. His fingers caught the edge just as a face appeared above him.

Reacting instantly, the ex-LAPD cop knotted his fist in the free-falling dreadlocks and yanked hard. With a yelp of pain and surprise, the Rastafarian came tumbling down hard against the rising lift. Wild-eyed and screaming, the Jamaican surged to his feet.

Lyons scrambled over the edge into a small stockroom lined with metal wire shelves and tried to bring the .45 into play. Before he had the chance, he heard Blancanales's H&K MP-5 cut loose. The Rastafarian crumpled.

Flailing his elbows and knees, Lyons made it into a standing position and raced through the open door at the back of the stockroom. The smell of gasoline, petroleum products and wax permeated the air.

Once through the door, Lyons found himself in an open car lot filled with gleaming automobiles. A scaled-down version of a hot-air balloon in a rainbow of colors floated in the blue afternoon sky from a corner post above a giant plastic Black Angus cow standing on a flatbed trailer. Four lanes of traffic drifted slowly through the intersection to the east, crossed by a two-lane street to the north.

Huge speakers tied into a common PA system addressed the potential crowd of auto buyers.

"Y'all c'mon in, folks," a twangy voice entreated over the PA system, "and see what kind of deals Okie Bob can cut you. Goats, boats, ropes, or anything that glitters—we'll take any kind of trade-in."

Three Rastafarians—one of them the main speaker from downstairs—were racing through the lines of cars toward the four-lane street. The thin scarecrow of a man dressed in jeans, a Western-styled jacket and a cowboy hat barely noticed them as he tried to wave in drivers. A large belt-buckle button on the jacket with neon purple letters proclaimed him to be Okie Bob.

Lyons charged toward his prey. Traffic was at a standstill for the moment, and the two DEA cars with magnetic cherries flashing on the roofs couldn't reach the dealership. The doors opened and disgorged three armed officers in DEA jackets.

Altering his course slightly, Lyons vaulted to the hood of a pink '59 Cadillac in the row behind the fleeing Rastafarians. Getting his feet under him, the big Able Team warrior jumped to the bed of a Dodge Ram pickup, heaved himself to the top of the cab and threw himself at the three men.

One of the Rastafarians saw him, pointed and screamed a warning to his comrades. One of the men tried to bring his gun around.

Lyons connected with the two of them in a flying tackle that smashed them all to the hot pavement. Stray bullets spiderwebbed the windshields of the Jeep and a midsized sedan closest to them. The big ex-cop lashed out with a foot and knocked the pistol from the man's grip as he tracked the free Jamaican.

Turning, the Rastafarian brought up his Ingram M-10, screaming obscenities.

Throwing his gun hand out and firing from the point, Lyons emptied the .45 automatic. The sound of the shots rang out above the traffic noise, drawing immediate attention. Caught by all three bullets, the Rastafarian jerked backward and dropped.

The gang's leader slammed an overhand right into Lyons's face as he struggled to get away. "Turn me loose, mon," the Rastafarian grunted, "or I'll kill you with my own two hands."

Lyons spit blood into the man's face and released the empty automatic. Using his peripheral vision, he saw the other guy yank a snub-nosed .38 from under his T-shirt. Lunging forward, the Able Team leader smashed an elbow into his adversary's face, then shook his hand to free the combat knife from its forearm sheath.

The gleaming blade sank to the hilt in the man's left eye, coring into the brain. One bullet whispered by Lyons's ear and ripped a side mirror from a nearby sedan. Motor control gone, the corpse slumped into death in spasmodic quivers.

The Rastafarian leader swung again. Lyons blocked the blow, aware of the jacketed ATF agents forming a loose circle around them.

Brushing aside another blow from the Rastafarian leader as they both got to their feet, Lyons dropped the knife, then hooked the man solidly under the short ribs. The Jamaican's lungs emptied with a whoosh. Grabbing his enemy by the jacket lapels, the ex-LAPD cop shoved the man against the blunt nose of a Jeep.

Lyons dropped the empty clip from the .45 and shoved a fresh one home. He placed the barrel against the Jamaican's forehead and pushed, pinning the man's head against the Jeep's hood and making him look up into the bright sky. The light hurt his eyes, drawing tears, and blood trickled from the corner of his mouth.

Lyons's voice was ice-cold when he spoke. "When I take this gun away, I want to hear the name of the man who brokered this deal. If I don't hear it, I put the barrel back and pull the trigger because you were resisting arrest. You got it?"

The man nodded.

Lyons pulled the gun back and waited.

"Allard Savitch."

"Where do I find him?"

"New York."

"That covers a lot of country." Lyons leaned in with the automatic.

"Queens. That's all I know. I swear." The Jamaican closed his eyes and held his hands palm-up.

Turning, Lyons addressed the nearest ATF officer. "Cuff him and sit on him in case I need to get back to him."

The ATF guy nodded and stepped forward, cuffs already open and hanging from his hand.

Lyons glanced at his teammates and O'Reilly. "What about Thone?"

"*Nada,*" Blancanales answered. "We confiscated his computer equipment."

"But it looks like it's already been hit with a virus and wiped clean," Schwarz added. "Chances are we're going to turn up empty there."

"Yeah." Lyons watched Okie Bob racing from damaged vehicle to damaged vehicle, extremely vocal in his disbelief. "I'll grab a phone and see if Barb and Aaron can work this thing from the other end. Money changing hands between Thone's people and the Rastafarians has got to leave a trail somewhere. Thone's going to run out of places to hide damn quick."

"—AS YET AREN'T SURE what millionaire industrialist, Hayden Thone's, involvement is with the events taking place at Fortress Arms's prestigious shooting range, Clay Pigeons."

Sitting on the hard bed in his hotel room, Thone rested his elbows on his knees and laced his fingers together as he watched the special news report. A glass of schnapps sat between his feet on the thin carpet.

The anchorwoman was lovely. Her olive complexion and Asiatic features made her look like a porcelain doll, though her hairstyle and clothing were clearly American. She was doing a thorough job of stretching the meager information the Department of Alcohol, Tobacco and Firearms had given her. A VCR, still with the purchase order taped to the front, sat on top the television, recording the broadcast.

Anger stirred in Thone as he gazed at the police barricade in front of the shooting range. A number of dreams were being dragged down in front of his eyes.

"Penny for your thoughts." Salvatore Mancuso stood near the curtained window, the fading light glowing around him. Noises from the swimming pool outside were punctuated with shrill children's voices. The accountant was overdressed for the hotel's usual clientele. His dark blue suit looked like a suit of armor.

Thone showed him a small smile. "I was just thinking that I'm going to miss the Hollywood crowd."

"I thought you despised them."

"For the most part, yes. But they are unmatched in their taste for arrogance and pompousness."

"You said that about the Brits."

"And I meant it. But the British are much too reserved." When the news broadcast wrapped, Thone used the remote control and rewound the tape to the beginning of the segment. "I like the way Hollywood can turn cannibalistic when the ratings come in. Watch this tape."

Mancuso crossed the room and studied the images on the television. "What am I looking for?"

"The leader of this group." Thone checked his watch. "Marney should be here soon."

"Yes." Mancuso pointed. "There. They list him for you. O'Reilly, of the ATF."

"He's a false front."

"You're sure?"

"I wouldn't say it otherwise." Thone took a sip of the schnapps and felt it burn along his throat. Three minutes later, he thought he'd identified the man he was looking for. Pressing the buttons on the remote, he rewound the segment twice more.

"The big blond man," Mancuso said.

"Yes."

"Do you know him?"

"No."

Someone knocked on the door, and Mancuso crossed the room to look through the peephole. An instant later he said, "It's Marney."

After checking the small Walther .22 in his coat pocket and making sure the silencer was firmly threaded on, Thone rose and walked to the VCR. He thumbed the Eject button and took out the tape. "Let him in."

Mancuso unbolted the door and stepped back, ushering in the new arrival.

Standing six feet tall and possessing a swimmer's build, Phil Marney could have easily been mistaken for Thone in a good light, except for his dark hair and eyes. The Fortress Arms CEO had found the man four years ago while working with an agency representing famous movie-star impostors. Cliff Janek, the owner of Doubles, Inc., had boasted that everyone had a twin somewhere. Thone had bet the man a thousand dollars that a twin couldn't be found for the Fortress Arms CEO. Ten days later, Janek had turned up someone whose resemblance to Hayden Thone was nothing short of uncanny.

After a brief interview, Thone had hired the man to help with security. Fourteen months later, Doubles, Inc. went out of business, along with any record of Phil Marney outside of Fortress Arms documents. Less than two months after that, Janek was dead, apparently the victim of a mugging. De Moray had been quick and thorough.

"Hello, Phil," Thone said with a generous smile, extending his hand.

Marney took the hand and managed a slightly perplexed expression. His dress was casual, an oxford shirt, twill pants and a denim jacket. He considered himself to be quite an actor. "What's up? Every time I watch TV or listen to the radio, I hear your name."

"A bad bit of business," Thone replied. "But it'll be over soon."

"Glad to hear it."

"Can I fix you a drink?"

"Sure. Scotch and soda."

"Of course." Thone walked to the bathroom. "In here. I'm afraid we're operating in something of a frontier at the moment."

Mancuso shut the door. "All in the interests of anonymity."

Marney shrugged and followed Thone into the bathroom. Once the actor had cleared the door, the Fortress Arms CEO grabbed him by the shirtfront and swung him toward the shower stall. Flailing, Marney tried to regain his balance, but his arm shattered the glass door of the shower and he fell through. Before the actor could recover, Thone pulled the Walther from his pocket and fired four times in quick succession. The silencer made the percussions sound like hollow pops in the small room.

"Is it done?" Mancuso asked.

"Yes." Thone surveyed the damage in the mirror. Blood spotted his face and clothing as he'd expected. Close kills always resulted in spatters. Taking the handkerchief from his breast pocket, he wet it and dabbed away the crimson stains.

"His passport?"

Thone checked through Marney's jacket without finding the document. He'd been paying Marney to act as a glorified representative of a holding company that wouldn't easily be connected to Fortress Arms. Marney had gone out of the country at least seven times a year for the past three years. One more trip out for Phil Marney wouldn't even draw notice.

Thone stood. "No passport, but I found his house key. We'll need to make a quick stop before we hit the airport."

"Are we leaving now?" Mancuso handed him a freshened drink.

"Not quite." Thone took the flip phone from the bed, opened it and punched in a number.

A flat, sibilant voice answered. "Cyber Realities. What's your number?"

Thone gave his identification number.

"How can I help you, Mr. Rickert?"

"I need the substitution done."

"How soon?"

"Now."

There was a click and a whir of computer noises. "It's done. My fee?"

Thone read off a Cayman Island banking number from memory.

"Okay," the voice replied. "The amount has been verified. You have a nice day."

Breaking the connection, Thone looked at Mancuso. "Now we can leave this country behind. All across the nation, Phil Marney's fingerprints have been switched for mine. In case I get stopped somewhere along the way."

"I wasn't aware that he had a record," Mancuso said.

"A two-year stint in the Oregon National Guard. They had his prints on federal files. Now they have mine. Probably I won't be bothered by any authorities, but this will lend further credibility to who I am if necessary."

"The hacker you used? Cyber Realities?"

"He hates bureaucracy. Trust me. I've had him checked out, and made certain he knows I have people he doesn't want to see come for him." Thone punched another number into the flip phone.

The recording was clear and concise, and gave the current stock exchange numbers on eight investment possibilities, then an advertisement for an airline.

At the end of the advertisement, Thone keyed in a nine-digit sequence, followed by a three-digit code. When he called the number again, the stock listings stayed the same, but the advertisement was for another major airline. Satisfied, he hung up.

"The Huntsman project?" Mancuso asked. He removed a two-gallon container of gasoline from the closet and uncapped it.

Thone nodded. "Terrorism across the globe is about to increase dramatically."

"Do you think that's wise?"

Thone looked at the man.

Mancuso turned up a palm. "No offense intended, Hayden, but you've gone to considerable time and expense to set up the Huntsman network. To needlessly expose it now, when it doesn't seem necessary—"

"I'll be the judge of what's necessary and what's not." Thone took the gas can from the Sicilian and walked into the bathroom. "Military intelligence came after me. There's another covert force out there, headed up by a man named Harold Brognola, who's even more dangerous than the Army personnel I encountered. If they knew enough to find me, I can only guess what Brognola and his people have put together."

"And a show of force will gain some time."

"Yes. Hopefully it will also confuse them." Thone took a tube of hair color from his pocket, squeezed some into his palm, then raked it through his hair with his fingers. In seconds, his image in the blood-spattered mirror became dark-haired. After he washed and dried his hands, he sluiced the gasoline over Marney's body and poured a trail out into the center of the room. The children's voices in the swimming pool remained shrill.

The carpet darkened as the last of the gasoline glugged into a deepening swamp. Finished with the can, he tossed the container into the corner. It didn't make any difference if the fire department found it on the premises; their fire inspectors would know how it got started. The important thing was that Marney's identity would probably be concealed at least for a time.

He took a last look around the room. Then, assured nothing incriminating was left behind, he took a package of motel matches from his pocket, struck one and waited for the rest to catch fire. Once the pack was blazing, he tossed it into the center of the gasoline puddle.

The fuel caught, eddying out in blue and yellow streams as the flames raced to follow the trail leading into the bathroom. By the time they reached the outer doors, a barely functional smoke alarm was tweeting a warning.

"Where do we go from here?" Mancuso asked as he slid behind the wheel of a Chevy sedan.

"Marney's house, and then Austria." Thone put on a pair of sunglasses and belted himself into the passenger seat. "The President will be heading to Jerusalem, and I want to watch."

"You're sure?"

He turned to the Sicilian and smiled. "I'm sure. I've got influence with a few Middle Eastern lobbying groups. I'll make a phone call to them and get the ball rolling. The President has made a big production of American involvement with the new peace treaties between the Palestinians and Israel. He won't pass up the chance to become a footnote in the history books." He drummed his fingers on the car's roof as Mancuso eased out of the small parking lot and into the flow of traffic. In the distance, he could hear the first of the fire-engine sirens. "He'll also get the chance to become the first President to be assassinated since Kennedy. Television coverage will be extensive. And once it's shown that the political head of the most powerful nation in the world isn't safe from terrorism, how can anyone else expect to be? I predict a huge munitions profit."

6

"You watching this?"

Mack Bolan glanced at the twenty-seven-inch television set mounted on the side of the Learjet. A montage of news scenes played in the four quadrants open on the screen. The television relay was from a satellite feed set up by Stony Man Farm from all across the world. Grimaldi communicated by intercom from the cockpit.

"Yeah," the warrior said as he poured another cup of coffee. The events in Italy had transpired hours ago. The members of Phoenix Force were making a short jump of their own with McCarter at the helm. Sally Coleman had been left with American military forces in Naples.

"You'd think every terrorist group in the world has suddenly gone nuts," the pilot said.

Bolan silently agreed. He made his way across the jet to the table and chairs set up opposite the television and took a seat. The Stony Man team had managed quick showers, a change of clothes and a bite to eat before using the transportation Price had arranged for them at Naples. Though feeling refreshed, fatigue had become a grim adversary. Once the briefing the Stony Man mission controller had called for was over, he intended to catch a few hours of rest on the flight back into the United States.

In the four broadcasts open to him, he watched stories unfold concerning terrorist attacks in Great Britain, Japan, France and Germany. He knew from earlier news reports that the Middle East was fast becoming a confusion of attack and counterattack between groups for and against the peace talks.

As he mentally considered and digested the information open to him, Bolan took out his war book and began making neat entries. There were already pages filled with tactical information—in his own brand of shorthand—along with suppositions he'd made about Thone's operation.

He used the remote control and flipped through the channels on the television. His attention captured by a station out of L.A. depicting violence in night-darkened streets, he used the remote to adjust the broadcast to fill the screen and bring up the volume. The tag gave the address as the South Central district.

Three cars were overturned and flaming in the streets, and two small apartment buildings had smoke streaming from the windows. Three police cars were parked haphazardly in the street as the uniformed officers took cover behind open doors. Shots rang out intermittently, punctuating the male reporter's comments. Fleet shadows raced between the buildings.

"—in the middle of a war zone here." The reporter was slim and Hispanic, dressed in a leather jacket, T-shirt and jeans. He hunkered behind the sheltering bulk of a van carrying the television station's markings. Obviously he hadn't been on duty when the violence broke out.

The cameraman moved nervously, shifting from the reporter to the street scene with jerking abandon. White letters suddenly materialized in the lower right corner, identifying the reporter as Ed Flores.

Without warning, Flores's face seemed to come apart on the screen, swelling until it burst. A crimson film covered the camera lens and oozed downward. A voice off-camera said, "Oh shit," and was followed almost immediately by retching sounds. The camera crashed to the ground and went off.

"That wasn't a stray round," Grimaldi said.

"No." Bolan recognized the handicraft of a sniper. "Someone's up on those buildings taking out targets that will garner the most attention." He didn't let the helpless feeling overtake him. He'd known since the beginning of his Everlasting War that he could prevent only some of the tragedies waiting at the hands of the cannibals living in the shadowy cracks of civilization. There were no ties to Thone regarding this violence yet, but he was sure the man's handiwork would be found in the design somewhere. Hayden Thone and his organization would pay.

The computer station in the corner of the Lear's workspace beeped for attention. Leaving his seat, the warrior went over and tapped the activation keys, bringing the communications link on-line.

"Striker." It was Barbara Price's voice. The line was being scrambled through Kurtzman's cybernetic systems.

"Here," he said.

"You've seen the news?"

"Yes."

"What's your view?"

"The sooner we take down Hayden Thone, the better."

The mission controller's face filled the television monitor. Honey blond with looks that had graced the covers of several magazines when she'd been younger, Barbara Price was nothing short of breathtaking. From the background around her, the warrior knew she was in her private office. "We still haven't made a connect to him."

"Able hit the Clay Pigeons offices?" Bolan asked.

"Yes, but their computer systems had already been crashed. We haven't recovered anything of value yet, but Akira's still sifting through the electronic debris. If something's there, he'll find it." She paused. "Just a minute. We're ready to link up with Phoenix and Able."

Bolan sipped his coffee and glanced at his watch. He was still hours from Miami and Brognola.

Two windows opened up on the television monitor, revealing Able Team in a darkened office and Phoenix Force—minus McCarter—in the belly of a jet similar to the Lear Bolan was in.

"I'm going to be brief," Price said. "Striker and Phoenix need to take advantage of the downtime, and Able has to make the jump to New York to follow up on a lead they uncovered that might give us another piece to work with."

Bolan pulled the war book closer and took up his pen.

"We know more about the Huntsman angle now," Price went on, "thanks to the efforts of Dr. Brookshaus."

Dr. Vivian Brookshaus was the specialist in mind control and multiple personalities that Price had enlisted to aid in the Huntsman research. She'd worked numerous cult deprogrammings for different American covert agencies.

"Apparently this is a further refinement of research the CIA has been involved with," the mission controller said. "It's been around for a while. A pretty little package called MK Ultra."

"I've heard something of it," Katzenelenbogen told them, "from Mossad resources. It had something to do with American servicemen being given drugs by prostitutes."

"Right," Price said. "On the surface, it looked like the sailors were the actual targets of the programming, but actually it was the prostitutes themselves. They were already living outside the rules of society, so they were easier to manipulate. From what I've been able to find out, the MK Ultra researchers were successful in their attempts, and were able to overlay personalities with other identities. The core personality, the actual person, doesn't know about the altered personalities, or alters, and actually becomes submerged during the process."

"That was what happened to Norman Hlabka?" Carl Lyons asked.

Bolan knew from progress reports that Lyons had been in contact with Hlabka's wife, who'd thought she'd been a widow for years. He knew from Lyons's report that the woman hadn't been faring well.

"Yes," Price answered. "Brookshaus has successfully peeled back four alters to reach the core personality. Hlabka's going to need a lot more therapy before he can take up a normal life again."

"You're saying the Huntsman personality was grafted onto these people?" Gary Manning asked.

"Every one of them," Price replied. "We're not sure how it was done. Hlabka has no memory of it. As far as he's concerned, it's still 1991."

Bolan knew part of the story from the brief stay he'd managed at Stony Man Farm before going into Italy to help retrieve Calvin James and the rear admiral's daughter.

"The grafted alters came from one man," Price said. "He's who we believe the Huntsman to really be." The screen cleared, then a picture of Alexander De Moray filled it. "This is Alexander De Moray. He's ex-Special Forces, ex-CIA, and chief enforcer for Fortress Arms. However this alter-transferring process is done, it's his personality that's grafted into these people."

"Fortress Arms?" Calvin James asked.

"Used to be called Festung Armor," Price said. "They were rivals of the Krupp family for the last four hundred years or so. The present CEO of the corporation is Hayden Thone. The company incorporated and moved to the L.A. area in 1980. You'll be getting in-depth dossiers on him and De Moray, as well as a handful of other people we've been able to tie to this operation."

"Who are these people?" David McCarter asked.

The screen cleared and returned to Price and the two windows. "Able Team managed the footwork on that end of things. We've been able to match up most of the confirmed Huntsman corpses with people thought to be dead for years. We've found out that in all cases, the individuals who later turned up claiming to be the Huntsman were ex-police officers or ex-military, who became detectives and security people."

"They were all involved in the private security sector when they were supposedly killed?" Rafael Encizo asked.

"Right. Each of these people supposedly won a free trip to Monte Carlo or another vacation spot in Europe. While they were at the casino, assassins broke in, killed some of them and obviously made off with preselected men and women."

"To subject them to Huntsman conditioning," Manning said.

Price nodded. "We think so."

"Why ex-cops?" James asked.

"Brookshaus has a theory that the police or military training made the people—at least the ones who became the Huntsman—more susceptible to the alter programming," Price said. "I'm inclined to agree. As I understand it, to frame an alter personality on an individual, a number of criteria must be met."

"Or it will reject the personality transplant," Blancanales said.

"Yes."

"These people who became the Huntsman," Katz interjected, "they were all individuals who were blooded as military or police?"

"We're through almost ninety percent of them," Price said, "and that appears to be the case."

"So they have a natural proclivity for violence," the Israeli went on.

"They're no strangers to it at any rate."

"The final bow on the whole package," Lyons said, "is that all the security outfits involved as employers of these people are owned through various fronts by Fortress Arms. As their employers, Thone had access to their dental records, which could be altered as needed to identify dead bodies brought to the sites where they were supposed to have been killed, and he had access to their MMPI tests."

"What's an MMPI?" Manning asked.

"Minnesota Multiphasic Personality Inventory," James answered automatically. Like Lyons, the ex-SEAL had been a cop for a time, as well.

"Psych records," Schwarz said in disgust. "Sounds like Thone was lining up a bunch of lab rats. Okay, we know Thone is responsible for the various incarnations of the unkillable Huntsman running around the globe, but we haven't answered what he's doing with them."

Price glanced at a notepad on the desktop beside her. "Judging from what we've uncovered, Thone has managed to place some of those Huntsman alters in a number of terrorist organizations under yet another alter. Most of them appear to be very high up in the hierarchy."

"You've identified some of them?" Katz asked.

"Aaron has. You'll get the specifics with the hard copy we're pushing your way." Price steepled her fingers in front of her face. "We're not sure what Thone is after at this point, but he's definitely in a position to pose a threat."

Bolan considered the flesh and blood robots Thone was responsible for, and all the death and mayhem that had resulted from Fortress Arms's illegal munitions deals and the counterfeit currency that had been pumped into international economies. "What's Thone's fiscal situation?"

"Fortress Arms is in trouble," Price answered. "Stocks had been dropping steadily since the passing of the Brady Bill. With Thone named as a fugitive today and the media's interest in the man, the bottom opened up on Wall Street. The corporation's not going to survive."

"Not the public one," the Executioner agreed. "But what about the empire Thone has built up behind the scenes?"

"We're still digging," Price replied. "Aaron tells me we might know more in the next few hours."

"You've seen the increase in terrorist attacks," Bolan pointed out. "Thone's alters have to be involved."

"The President is inclined to agree with you, but we're uncertain where to start."

"The Middle East is sure to be a target," Katz said. The Executioner was certain the Phoenix Force leader hadn't forgotten the near disaster that had struck in Jerusalem only a few days ago while Phoenix Force had been in the trenches to prevent it. "The new peace talks are still viable, even if only marginally so."

"Jerusalem might be hotter than you think, Yakov," Price said. "I'm getting some rumors from my White House feelers that the Man has been invited to take part in the negotiations."

"At this point," the Israeli stated, "I don't think that would be a good idea."

"Political pressure is intense now," Price said. "So I want Phoenix Force on hand in Jerusalem. Not as a pacifistic effort, though. Your team is going in hard. Aaron's group has come up with some solid connections between Fortress Arms and a number of the Palestinian splinter cells."

"The Bloody Wind?" McCarter asked hopefully.

"Is among them, and targeted," Price responded. "Stateside, Able is going to be tracking the money Clay Pigeons was raking in through the back door. Striker, I want you in Miami. Jack can keep a jet ready at Miami International Airport in case we find another direction for you to go. But someone's sold out Hal down there, and I have the feeling Thone's hand can't be far from the witches' brew developing there."

"What about the counterfeiting efforts?" Encizo asked.

"Purely economic terrorism," Bolan said. "I'd say it was aimed at destabilizing Third World governments that are getting financial help from the U.S. With the world economy in the shape that it is, widespread counterfeiting could create increased inflation and paranoia that could collapse some governments."

"Makes you want to go back to the days of burying your extra cash in mason jars in the backyard," Schwarz said.

"And maybe your neighbor with it," Lyons added grimly.

"Gentlemen," Price addressed them, "you have your assignments. If there are no further questions, I'm done."

Each of the Stony Man teams signed off and pulled out of the com link. Bolan stared at the television screen as it returned to the four views of world news. Hayden Thone's Huntsman alters had been carefully stacked throughout the world like dominoes. The design was elaborate and cruel, combining fear and paranoia into an archetype geared for destruction.

Even finding and removing Thone and the evil that Fortress Arms had wrought wouldn't guarantee those dominoes wouldn't fall in the confusion. A lot of innocent lives could still be lost. And protecting those lives was what the warrior had devoted nearly his entire existence to.

Miami, Florida

THE CALL CAME EARLY. Glancing through the haze of hard sunshine piercing the half-inch space above the curtains in the hotel room, Hal Brognola shifted on the hard bed and scooped up the strident instrument before it could ring again. He blinked and took a breath, automatically logging the time as 6:48 a.m.

"Hope I didn't wake you," the President of the United States said in a jovial voice.

"Ever vigilant." Brognola checked the nightstand beside the bed and found his snub-nosed .38 in its holster, a partial package of antacid tablets and two fresh rolls.

"Me, too." The President stifled a yawn.

"You up early or up all night?"

"All night. Sorry I didn't get back to you sooner, but things have been busting out all over."

"I know. I've been keeping up with the news and with reports from the Farm." Brognola pushed himself out of bed and stumbled to the pot of coffee he'd had room service bring up less than three hours earlier. Despite the caffeine, he'd slept fully clothed for the past two hours, but it had been one long nightmare after another. His eyes burned with fatigue.

"From your message, I gather things there have reached an impasse."

"To put it mildly." The big Fed poured fresh coffee into a half-empty cup. There wasn't much coffee in the pot, and room service was so incredibly slow he didn't want to try ordering another. "George Cosgrove is probably busy rounding up a lynch mob."

"He's the Treasury guy."

"Yeah." Brognola crossed the room to the window and used a forefinger to move the curtain slightly. He was twenty-seven stories up and facing Biscayne Bay, so the threat of a sniper was slim. Still, he made it a practice to never take chances he didn't need to.

"What's his beef?"

"He tripped to some of the sensitive information I'd disseminated to the Stony groups."

"How?"

"I'm not certain. Barb has checked into it enough to realize that it looks like someone clued him in. No other way could he get his hands on a few of the documents he has."

"Any idea who?"

"No."

The President was silent for a moment. "Where does this leave you?"

"To put it bluntly, with my ass hanging out."

"What about the other international teams?"

"Sir, the cop isn't made who likes being held out on by someone who's supposed to be working with him. Cosgrove asks, they'll probably give him the rope and plant the tree. In my opinion, my usefulness here is over. If you've paid attention to the news, you know some of the media is starting to link my actions to your office in a very unfavorable light."

"It's another damn fiasco. God, I'm getting tired of them." The President sighed. "Look, Hal, maybe you can do something in the way of damage control while you're down there. Give it another twelve, fourteen hours at most, and you can bail."

"All right. But at ten o'clock tonight, I'm going to pull the rip cord on this operation. I can be of more help at Stony Man."

"By then, maybe the Stony Man teams will have a better handle on this thing."

There was nothing Brognola could say, so he didn't.

"One other thing," the President said.

"Yeah."

"I'm leaving for Jerusalem in twenty minutes. I've been invited to take part in the peace talks."

Brognola let his breath out between his teeth. "I don't think that's the safest thing you can do." He returned to his bed and felt through his jacket pockets until he found a cigar. He stuck it in his mouth and clamped down on it.

"Maybe not," the Man replied, "but I've got a riot escalating in L.A. that might rival the Rodney King protest, and heads of state in Third World nations we've been building relations with who are suddenly wondering if this country can provide as much protection as I've promised. I don't see that I have much of a choice if I want my stance on international matters to be respected."

Brognola knew the President was right. With the machinations Thone and Fortress Arms had created, there was a lot on the line concerning America's image as protector. The world was growing smaller, and at no other time had the United States been in more of a position to positively affect geopolitical events. That position couldn't be sacrificed.

"Ms. Price tells me that Phoenix Force is already on the ground in Jerusalem," the President said. "I couldn't be in more capable hands."

"I know." Brognola crunched two of the antacid tablets. "In that case, I'll wish you Godspeed and good luck." When the President broke the connection, the big Fed hoped that was enough. Then he drained the cup of coffee and walked to the shower. He had a feeling the day wasn't going to go well, and he didn't see the sense of delaying it any longer than necessary. Before he reached the door, he stopped and returned to the bedside for the holstered handgun. Carrying it with him into the bathroom helped.

7

"He's coming."

The Huntsman studied her reflection in the gift shop's plate-glass window, fronting the hotel lobby, as she listened to the voice coming through the earphone she wore. She was dressed in a Hawaiian print sundress that left little to the imagination. Open-toed sandals encased her feet, and her face was somewhat disguised by a floppy straw hat and large sunglasses in case Brognola remembered her from the restaurant the previous day. A Detonics .45 was hidden in the knit handbag at her side.

Though etched in black and white, with the colors washed out due to the plate-glass window, the Huntsman found her image unsettling. Confusing thoughts cascaded through her mind, bringing headaches in pulsing waves. Tiny beads of perspiration dotted her upper lip, and her hand trembled as she swept a lock of her auburn hair away from her face.

On the other side of the window, the blue-haired saleswoman finished hanging T-shirts with Miami Dolphin logos and tourist price tags on them. The Huntsman turned, feeling the presence of the *other* swirling through the mind they shared. She slipped a hand inside the knit bag and closed her fingers around the butt of the Detonics. The metal felt cool and hard.

The Huntsman and the *other* had both been in situations like this one before. Even though the adrenaline level was up, her nerves were steady. She didn't know who the backup team was, or how many of them were involved in the present operation, but she knew she could trust them. Spots swam in front of her eyes, but she ignored them until they faded.

"Where is Brognola?" the Huntsman asked into the minimike.

"The stairs. East side."

Turning, the Huntsman changed her line of sight, spotting the Justice Department man halfway down the winding stairway. Adrenaline had kicked her senses into high gear, allowing her a more clear focus.

Brognola looked tired and absently worked at the tie around his neck. His suit was gray and cut so the pistol riding his hip wouldn't be noticeable to the untrained eye. The quiet, rebellious part of the Huntsman's mind screamed that Brognola was a cop, that she could read it in the way the man carried himself and the way his eyes moved around the lobby. But the Huntsman didn't care. Her heart rate increased, followed by respiratory levels as her body geared up to go into action.

"Take him," the male voice in her ear instructed. "Take him before he gets out of the lobby."

The Huntsman moved forward, fighting against the *other* that shouted in the back of the shared mind. The pressure of the headache increased. For a moment, double vision threatened, compounded by a sense of vertigo.

A hand fell on the Huntsman's shoulder.

"Honey," a soft voice said.

The Huntsman turned and found the saleswoman from the gift shop standing behind her.

"Are you all right?" the saleswoman asked.

"You're going to miss him, damn it," the voice in her ear insisted. "Take the shot."

Over the saleswoman's shoulder, she spotted the tall man with dark hair and piercing blue eyes. She recognized him as a warrior at once. The Huntsman part of her brain identified him as a potential threat, but was confused because the man might be one of the backup team on the play.

"I'm fine," she told the saleswoman, gently disengaging the hand from her shoulder. Before the woman could say anything more, the Huntsman turned and saw that Brognola had passed her, heading for the double entrance doors.

Through the glass, the harsh morning sunlight bounced from the windshields and chrome parts of the sluggish flow of traffic. There was no doorman. Limned by the light coming in from outside, the Department of Justice man was a perfect target.

The Huntsman summoned Brognola's first name from memory with effort. The *other* was struggling for motor nerve control. "Hal," she called in a voice that sounded desperate to her.

Brognola halted with one hand on the door, then turned to face her. He looked perplexed and guarded.

The words that filled her conscious mind were those of an old friend, but she couldn't remember who the friend was. They reminded her that she was the Huntsman and that the Huntsman could never be killed. She felt euphoric, and most of the confusion dropped away as she brought the Detonics .45 from the handbag.

HIS COMBAT SENSES FLARING, Mack Bolan raced across the hotel lobby toward the woman pointing the pistol at Brognola. He'd noticed her interest in the big Fed only a few seconds before, and had started making his way toward her when she pulled the weapon. Her hesitant movements had warned him that she was one of the Huntsman alters, and—from everything Price and Kurtzman had turned up—one of the innocents. The .44 Desert Eagle was in his hand, but he didn't want to use it.

She noticed him just before the pistol was leveled at Brognola. Her head swiveled toward him, and for an instant she appeared to be undecided. The hesitation earned the Executioner another step.

Around them in the lobby, guests started screaming and fleeing from the immediate vicinity. A bellboy scattered a load of luggage, and the bags skittered across the floor until they knocked over a rubber palm tree near the phone booths.

The woman tried to fall back into a defensive stance and bring the pistol around to face Bolan.

Launching himself at her the last few feet, the Executioner caught the woman around the waist in a flying tackle that dropped them both to the tiled floor. He straddled her and struck a blow that caught her gun wrist and sent the weapon flying.

"Striker!" Brognola yelled, drawing his .38 from his holster.

Then gunfire crackled and filled the lobby, echoing cavernously in the enclosed space.

Hammered backward, the big Fed crashed through the double entrance doors. Glass shattered and fell in shards around him.

Managing the woman with one hand as she struggled against him, the Executioner swept the room with a glance. He identified three of the attackers and knew from his previous encounters with the Huntsman alter that they

belonged to the backup team in the field to either aid the
alter or recover the body.

The big .44 came up in his hand automatically. Bolan
dropped the sights over the chest of the man firing from
behind the glass-walled atrium holding salt-white drift-
wood and deep purple orchids. The warrior fired three
rounds. The atrium glass blew apart, and the gunner was
torn from his position to go sprawling across the floor.

The second attacker was in a kneeling position near the
bank of telephones. He had his gun hand crossed over his
other wrist, his eyes as hard as bearings over his sights as
he aimed at Bolan.

Rolling to one side, the Executioner yanked the woman
after him. He caught sight of the dagger as she slipped it
free of a thigh sheath under her short skirt. He released his
hold on her and narrowly avoided her attack as he continued rolling. The sharp point of the dagger stabbed into the
tile and chipped pieces free.

On his back, shooting with both hands to maintain ac-
curacy, the Executioner fired a double punch of 240-grain
boattails that took the second man in the face and kicked
him backward. He got to his feet just as the woman came
for him, a silent tigress with one bared and deadly fang.

The remaining member of the backup team was working as one of the hotel staff. He stood in front of the
Spanish galleon clock that took up most of the wall behind the desk, utilizing the cover provided by the cash
register. He tripped the magazine release and dropped an
empty clip, a fresh one ready in his hand.

Taking advantage of the brief respite, Bolan side-
stepped the woman's attempt to stab him in the throat. He
used his empty hand to make contact with her wrist and
further deflected the knife. Off balance, she couldn't defend herself against his clenched backfist. His knuckles

brushed her jaw, and she went out on her feet. The dagger clattered away.

When he turned his attention back to the last attacker, Bolan saw the man's target had shifted. Instead of the Executioner, the gunner was aiming at the woman. Without hesitation, the warrior loosed the remaining rounds in the Desert Eagle. They all caught the gunner between collarbone and waist, driving him backward into the ship clock and bringing it down.

The Executioner ejected the empty magazine, rammed a new one home and tripped the slide release.

He fixed the head desk clerk with a drill-sergeant's glare. "Call the police. Now!"

"Yes, sir." The man moved toward the phone, stepping over the corpse. No one else appeared ready to move.

Remembering how fast Brognola had gone down under the gunfire, Bolan crossed the lobby to the broken doors. Glass shards crunched underfoot as he neared his fallen friend. Out in the street a handful of cars had stopped, blocking free traffic flow.

"Shit," Brognola groaned as he blinked his eyes and reached for his midsection. Rips in his shirt showed where the bullets had struck.

"You okay?" Bolan asked, maintaining a defensive position. He could see the Kevlar vest under the big Fed's shirt. Relief uncoiled some of the tensed muscles inside him. It was never easy seeing a friend fall to enemy guns, and the Executioner had witnessed his share.

"Better than I would have been." Brognola groaned and grimaced as he sat up. He hooked three fingers through bullet holes in his shirt. "Damn, that was close."

"Other side of the grave, pal," the Executioner said, offering a hand and helping the man up.

"Barb told me you'd be around." Brognola dusted broken glass from his clothing carefully. "Didn't know it would make a difference this soon. What about the wrecking crew?"

Bolan holstered the Desert Eagle on his hip under the tails of the leather coat. "Three of them. They're down."

"The lady?"

"Alive. I think she's one of the Huntsman alters. The vest stopped the bullets, but did they break anything?"

Brognola shook his head. "I don't believe so. The locals are going to be all over this thing in short order. It might be better if they didn't get hold of the woman."

"If I take her out of here, there's plenty of witnesses to tell the police about it. You stay behind, you're going to bear the brunt of the investigation."

"No problem. The Man has already pulled me from this thing. By tonight, I'll be history in Miami. I can face the heat until then. If she can give us something, we need it. The sooner we get Hayden Thone run to ground, the sooner we can put this behind us."

Bolan nodded. As liaison for the Stony Man Farm group, Brognola had weathered his share of political storms in the past. It was the big Fed's battlefield, and he knew the flash zones. The cover Kurtzman provided was in the Michael Belasko name under the Justice Department umbrella. The alias was an old name that carried a good history and would stand up to most investigations, but there was no reason to take the added risk of anyone finding out who Bolan really was.

"You better get moving," Brognola said.

"Sure." Conscious of the stares coming his way, the warrior reentered the hotel lobby. Producing a pair of disposable handcuffs, he cuffed the woman, then went through her handbag.

"ID?" Brognola asked. He stood behind the Executioner and rubbed his ribs tenderly.

"None."

"The other guys?"

"Haven't checked." Bolan stood and pulled the unconscious woman with him. He settled her weight easily over one broad shoulder and strode toward the door.

"I find something, I'll let Barb know."

"Do that." Bolan glanced out at the traffic. The street in front of the hotel was blocked, though both streets at either end appeared to still be moving without problem. His car was parked in an underground garage almost four blocks away. When the first sounds of sirens whined in the distance, he figured he didn't have time to try for it. And, even if this was Miami, walking down the sidewalk with a woman over his shoulder wasn't going to go unnoticed.

A large Hispanic man with a shaved head stepped in front of the warrior. "Hey, man, put that woman down."

Bolan didn't slow, but reached inside his jacket pocket, found the Justice credentials Price'd had waiting for him and gave the ID a workout. "It's under control here," he said, making heavy eye contact.

The man raised his hands and stepped back.

At the corner, Bolan hooked his fingers in his mouth and whistled. The noise was almost lost among the keening sirens, and he guessed that the average person wouldn't have known the difference.

However, the cabdriver in the refurbished aquamarine-and-white Studebaker sedan did. Arm hanging out the window, the cabbie cut across two lanes of oncoming traffic and pulled to a stop with three tires on the sidewalk, interfering with pedestrian passage.

Without preamble, Bolan opened the rear door and dropped the woman inside, then slid in beside her.

"She sick?" the cabbie asked.

"Something like that."

"She's not going to barf is she?" He adjusted the rearview mirror.

Bolan reached into his jacket pocket and took out five one-hundred-dollar bills. He fanned them, tore them in two and handed over half of the bills.

"Doesn't matter," the cabbie declared as he tucked his half into his vest pocket.

The sirens sounded louder. Bolan leaned forward. "I need to get to the airport the fastest way you know how. If we get stopped by the police, you lose your bonus."

"You rob a bank or something?"

"No, but they're going to ask you questions."

The cabbie dropped the transmission into gear and bolted through the first opening in the traffic, drawing a half-dozen angry honks. His gaze cut nervously to the rearview mirror. "I can keep my mouth shut, man. You ask anybody that knows me. Ain't no reason for you to kill me when we get to where we're going."

"I don't intend to kill you," Bolan said easily. "Watch the traffic."

The cabbie swerved around a fruit truck into the oncoming lane for a moment, then cut back into traffic.

"I kill you when we get to where we're going, I might as well hang out a neon sign. Right?"

"Right. So what should I tell the cops?"

"Everything you can remember. It won't matter." The cabbie flew by Orange Bowl Stadium and made the turn onto Highway 836. Less than a mile ahead of them was the toll station. The warrior knew if they made the toll, they had a clear shot into Miami International Airport where Jack Grimaldi was standing at the ready with the Lear.

Without warning, the woman lunged for him, awkward with her hands handcuffed behind her back. Bolan got a hand up in time to hold her off, bare inches away. Her teeth snapped together and grazed the skin of his throat, drawing blood.

"You can't stop me," she said in a harsh voice, continuing to struggle against him. She managed to kick his shins painfully. "If you kill me, I only come back. The Huntsman cannot die. The Wild Hunt continues!"

Wrapping his arms around her and manhandling her with some difficulty, Bolan applied a sleeper hold just as the cabbie threw correct change into the toll bin. The Studebaker slipped under the rising bar just as the woman melted in the warrior's arms. When Bolan glanced forward, his eyes locked with those of the cabbie in the rearview mirror.

The man swallowed hard, but said nothing.

Bolan adjusted the woman's posture and made her as comfortable as he could. Her jaw was already turning blue from where he'd hit her. There was no guilt; he'd done what he had to do. But she was a reminder of the innocents that stood between the Stony Man teams and Fortress Arms. He wished that there was a guarantee that the deprogrammer Price had enlisted to aid them could help her, but he knew there wasn't. However, there *would* be a reckoning.

8

New York

Carl Lyons parked the van bearing the Sassan Tree Removal logo off the service road that ran behind the big houses in an elegant section of Queens. He slid on the earthroat headset and tapped the transmit button. "Pol. Gadgets."

"Here," Blancanales responded. "The front of the house looks clear. There are two hardguys standing on the veranda, but I've seen no sign of Savitch."

"I've got one door open on the garage," Schwarz said. "Savitch's driver is out, going over the Mercedes. Looks like he's planning a road trip today."

"I hope it's not something real pressing, because he's not going to make it." Lyons checked his gear under the loose tan coverall. The Colt Government Model was in shoulder leather with four spare clips. He took up the L-shaped fighting stick from the passenger seat and fitted it to one of the loops on the coverall, then hit the door release and stepped out into the misty morning.

Price and Kurtzman had turned up a wealth of information on Savitch from New York's Organized Crime Bureau and the FBI. Savitch had been covertly investigated by four different law-enforcement agencies, nine times in the past five years. None of the investigations had turned up anything that had led to a successful prosecution. Only once had any of the charges resulted in a court appearance by Savitch. Two of the witnesses had turned up dead while in protective custody, and the third had denied ever seeing the man before, stating for the record a description that in no way fit Savitch.

Judging from the elegant two-story home Savitch owned in Queens, brokering illicit deals in arms and drugs paid extremely well.

One way or another, Savitch's career was coming to a flaming halt today. After the Rastafarian gave up the broker, Price had requested and received federal no-knock warrants for Savitch's business and home addresses.

The Able Team warrior walked to the back of the van, pulling on a ballcap to cover the headset. He opened the rear of the van.

"They've got you spotted, Ironman," Blancanales radioed.

"How interested are they?" Lyons took a leather safety belt from a hook on the van wall, a hand saw from the selection on the cart before him and large pruning shears from a drawer. The special equipment case needed to gain access to the house had a shoulder strap which he shrugged into.

"They're lighting up. Must be a coffee break."

"Can't forget," Schwarz pointed out, "that Savitch probably knows the Rastafarian deal in L.A. went south. He might be expecting company and put his guys on alert."

Lyons closed the van doors and walked to the rear fence of the broker's property. A large, gnarled oak tree twisted toward the gray sky. Half of it was dead and jutted from the lightning-blasted trunk.

"Okay," Blancanales said in a tight voice, "it looks like they're only watching you for nuisance value."

The lower branches of the tree were easily navigated, and Lyons climbed smoothly. Thirty feet up, he halted and brought out the saw. The keen edge bit into a dead branch easily. Seconds later the limb dropped toward the ground amid a whirl of sawdust.

The mist gathered on his face where it wasn't protected by the ballcap. He squinted through the drizzle as he worked on another dead limb. If anyone in the house called the power company to check him out, they'd find a work order for the tree-trimming among the records. Kurtzman's hand was deft and thorough.

Three minutes passed and Lyons moved carefully among the rain-slick branches, edging closer to the power line that ran from the pole to the second-story roof of the house. The intervening distance was something over a hundred feet. A white gazebo trimmed in yellow sat about halfway between, and a sculpted rose garden was on the right. The trees and bushes had been placed carefully, then landscaped so they wouldn't pose problems for the security systems.

When he reached a height that he judged to be at least ten feet above the second-story roof, he tapped the transmit button on the headset. "How much attention am I drawing now?"

"*Nada,*" Blancanales said.

"Terrific," Lyons said as he shrugged out of the equipment case and balanced it across two limbs. "Then let's get this done."

"You say when," Blancanales replied.

Lyons clicked open the latches on the case and took out the compressed-air rifle from foam inserts. The three pieces fitted smoothly together and locked into place easily. He peered through the foliage of the living branches at the house, made sure he was still unnoticed, then screwed the CO_2 canister into place and charged the pneumatic system.

The steel dart he fitted into the barrel of the air rifle was eight inches in length and made of airplane alloys. Dark and hard-edged, it possessed a wedge-shaped head that would bite deep into wood, brick or stone. A nylon rope was secured through the eye in the dart's shaft. Two hundred feet of slack lay neatly curled in the well of the equipment case.

Lyons settled the rifle on his shoulder, took aim at the chimney on top of the second floor and squeezed the trigger. Recoil shoved against him as the anchor hurtled from the barrel. The hollow *thunk* of it striking home was audible for just a moment.

One of the guards stepped to the back of the house and looked up. An instant later he reached under his jacket and yelled for his partner's attention.

Lyons grabbed the trailing end of the nylon rope, wrapped some of it around the tree trunk where it would hold his weight, pulled tight and tied it with a hurried half hitch. He hit the transmit button, said, "I'm blown," then unstrapped the leather safety belt from his hips.

Both of the guards moved into the backyard carrying guns, one of them speaking rapidly into a radio handset.

Gripping one end of the leather belt, Lyons tossed it across the nylon rope and caught the free end in his other hand. He stepped from his perch just as the lead man started yelling for him to climb down from the tree.

The leather belt slid over the nylon rope as if it were greased. Lyons drew up his legs into a ball to present a smaller target. Zipping by below him and off to the right, the two men fired at the Able Team Leader from less than forty feet away. He saw one of them suddenly pitch forward onto his face a heartbeat before the piercing crack of Blancanales's Beretta M-21 sniper rifle rang out. The 7.62 mm rounds packed a lot of foot-pounds when they hit their target.

Then the bay windows of the great room suddenly glittered before him. Lyons braced himself for the impact. The delicate frames burst apart at once, and the impact-resistant glass shattered in all directions.

Off balance but through the bay window, Lyons swung wildly and managed to turn himself as the leather belt snapped taut against the window frame. For a moment he thought his arms were going to be jerked from their sockets as his forward momentum ended. Then he slammed into the inside wall, not leaving him enough breath to curse, with the pain that assailed him in spite of the body armor he wore under the coverall.

He grabbed the edge of the window frame and released the safety belt. Footsteps sounded from below, drumming quickly against the hardwood floor. He waited, knowing Blancanales would be hitting the front door and Schwarz would take care of the garage.

"Door," Blancanales radioed.

"Do it," Lyons replied, letting himself down the wall as far as possible. Even with his arms out all the way, he was still more than ten feet above the ground floor.

The prepared C-4 charge Blancanales had for the front door erupted with a thunderous clap.

Taking advantage of the diversion, Lyons let go his hold. He hit the floor just as an armed man spotted him. The first bullet missed the Stony Man warrior by inches and ripped plaster from the vaulted wall of the great room.

Automatically he went into a parachute roll. The gunner put two more rounds into the floor, searching for him.

Coming up on his hands and one leg, the ex-LAPD cop lashed out with his free foot and connected with his opponent's kneecap, creating a grating crack of bone.

The man fell, screaming and clutching at his injured leg.

On his feet, Lyons swung a boot at the writhing man's head, the impact driving the guy into unconsciousness. The Able Team leader reached into the coverall and drew the Colt Government Model. Clasping it in both hands in a modified Weaver stance, he moved through the house.

Crossing the great room, he walked through the door on the left leading out to the hall. At the door, sweeping clockwise, he commanded a view of the doors to the breakfast room, the foyer, the living room and the study. All were open.

A red-faced, barrel-chested man came through the breakfast-room door less than three feet away. Egg stained his sweater, but his hands never faltered on the cutdown shotgun he tried to bring up.

Lyons fired two rounds at point-blank range and the man went away. "Pol."

"Yeah. I'm moving into the dining room. As soon as I make the kitchen, I've got the upstairs covered."

Lyons walked toward the living room. To his right, between the two doors leading into the great room, a huge fish tank had been mounted into the wall. Colorful fish darted and swam, agitated by the vibrations of noise echoing into their environment. "Gadgets?"

"The garage is secure and both vehicles have been disabled. The driver didn't want to play. If you hear footsteps behind you, make sure it's not me before you cut loose."

"Right."

Movement at the threshold to the living room alerted Lyons. His reflexes saved his life. Dropping into a crouch as he recognized the barrel of a Glock 17, he brought the .45 into target acquisition.

The Glock jumped slightly five or six times as the gunner made the effort to take the Able Team warrior down. One of the 9 mm rounds slammed into Lyons's Kevlar vest with enough force to make him wince. At least two other bullets crashed into the aquarium. Fish, water, plants and colored gravel cascaded onto the floor.

Taking more deliberate aim, Lyons placed a round into the man's exposed shoulder. The 230-grain bullet ripped the attacker from his position, allowing the big ex-cop a follow-up shot to the head that put the man down. He pulled a Thunderflash grenade from a pocket, yanked the pin and underhanded the bomb into the living room. It bounced off the opposite wall, then Lyons looked away. The detonation sounded horrendous inside the room.

Lyons pushed himself up and sprinted to the doorway, keeping the double doors to the study covered at the same time. Three men were inside trying to recover from the effects of the blast. All were armed and saw Lyons at the same instant. Bullets chipped the wooden door frame and pocked holes in the walls.

Extending his arm around the door, Lyons took aim and squeezed the trigger. The first two rounds took the nearest man in the chest and ended the threat of the MAC-10 he carried. The next two bullets ripped holes through the low coffee table in front of the plush couch as the second target dived for cover. Tripping the magazine eject, Lyons coiled behind the door frame, took a fresh clip from his shoulder harness and fed it into the Colt.

"Ironman."

Lyons glanced up and saw Schwarz coming toward him, a Calico assault pistol with attached rifle stock in his hands. The Calico was one of the fiercest new urban weapons Lyons had ever seen, and Able Team had started to use them. The octagonal magazine on top of the pistol held one hundred 9 mm parabellum rounds.

"Could you use a broom?" Schwarz asked, falling into line beside Lyons.

"Yeah. Two guys. Armed with machine pistols, toward the back of the room."

Schwarz gave a short nod, then wheeled around the door and unleashed the Calico on full-auto. Brass flicked out and spun mad cartwheels before dropping to the hardwood floor. At least one round from the enemy guns caught Schwarz in the abdomen and shoved him backward. The Kevlar vest kept it from digging into flesh. He let off the trigger and stepped into the room.

Closing in behind his teammate, Lyons peered over Schwarz's shoulder. The living room looked like it had been redone by an interior decorator from hell. Fine pottery had been reduced to chips and splinters, and the furniture wouldn't have been fit for a fire sale. Both gunmen were sprawled across the floor.

"Clear," Schwarz said grimly.

Lyons took point and moved quickly for the study. Both doors were shut, and when he tried them, he found them locked. He stepped back and rammed them with his shoulder. The lock shattered with a clear, metallic ping. Using the momentum he'd already built up, he charged into the room, registering the three men and one woman gathered around the desk to his right at the far end. Allard Savitch sat at the computer keyboard.

"Kill the son of a bitch," Savitch ordered, then grabbed the arm of the slim brunette standing at his side and pulled her under the desk with him.

The two bodyguards started to move, then Schwarz backed Lyons's play, gliding easily into the study. The taller guard shook his head, then held his hands up, his pistol hanging from a finger. "I don't think so, Mr. Savitch."

"Count me out, too," the other man added, placing his gun on the desktop. "You want them shot, you shoot them yourself."

"Down," Lyons said, waggling the .45's barrel at the floor. Both men lay facedown on the floor and didn't offer any resistance when Schwarz came forward to cuff them. Lyons walked around the desk holding the Colt Government Model in both hands. "Come out. I see anything in the way of a threat, I'll shoot a big piece of you that will hurt for a long time but not interfere with your ability to talk. You understand?"

Savitch slowly stood, but kept the woman between himself and Lyons's pistol. "I want my lawyer, and I want to see the warrant you have to invade my home."

Lyons took the folded document from inside the coveralls and passed it over. At the computer console, Schwarz was busy replacing the regular modem with a scrambler modem he'd brought with him. "This is your lucky day," the big ex-cop said. "I'm not after you. You're just a small fish. If you can help me close the distance to Hayden Thone and the Fortress Arms gunrunning operation, you won't even have to carry the weight on this thing."

"Those are private records," Savitch protested as files started to scroll across the computer monitor.

Lyons knew Kurtzman was working his magic from Stony Man Farm. "Not anymore."

9

Jerusalem

"We're clean and green, people, so let's do it."

Yakov Katzenelenbogen glanced through the dirty windshield of the car at Jaffa Gate and the Citadel of David just beyond. He tapped the transmit button on the earthroat headset. "Move out, and stay in communication."

McCarter acknowledged, and the raucous thrum of his motorbike carried over the frequency. Encizo was clear and concise, and the Israeli knew the Cuban would keep covert watch from his position near the Dome of the Rock. James maintained watch over Solomon's Stables, the team's objective. Manning was behind the wheel of the car.

Katz hit the door release and stepped out into the harsh sunlight. Slipping on a dark pair of sunglasses, he shouldered a canvas rucksack with an attached camera bag. He wore jeans, joggers and a khaki shirt with long sleeves that appeared out of place in the heat, but disguised the straps that attached his prosthesis to his right arm. Instead of the hook, he wore the simulacrum of a human hand. Inside the hand was a specially modified .22 pistol. The clothing was close enough to a tourist look that he wouldn't get much attention as he passed through the streets of Jerusalem's Old City.

Gary Manning moved quietly behind Katz. Like the Israeli, he carried a rucksack containing the necessary equipment for the mission. The sun had already lent a coppery red undertint to his skin. He wore hiking boots, jeans and a denim shirt with the sleeves hacked off. The statement was obviously North American, and Katz could pass as his guide if asked.

As always, Katz felt the history of bloodshed, struggle and rapture that pervaded the city stretching out around him. He'd written articles on the geography and the past that had built this city, from the scholarly level to the voice of the people living on the streets, addressing the political and religious events that had given Jerusalem form and substance.

"What's on your mind?" Manning asked.

"Remembering," Katz answered as they walked through the citadel gate built by Suleiman the Magnificent in the sixteenth century.

"Seems to be a place for it." Manning swiveled his head as they walked through the narrow streets.

Dust swirled up from the remains of the empty moat as they crossed the bridge. An older man led a donkey bearing two chicken coops, a sack of vegetables and a little girl with a shy, snaggle-toothed grin under a mop of dark hair.

"This land," Katz said, "has long been torn by violence. I have fought for it for years. When I was younger, I thought maybe I would see a kind of peace in my lifetime. Now, I really wonder if that is possible."

"It won't be as long as Hayden Thone is allowed to run free," Manning said.

Katz led the way through the Armenian Quarter, winding through the twisting lanes and Oriental souks, and up and down the steep stairways. The air was cooler under the shadowy, covered passageways between buildings.

The Stony Man Farm cybernetic teams had turned up further information on the Bloody Wind terrorist group through the files recovered from Clay Pigeons. Tokaido had been able to restructure a number of them. Many of the pieces were still missing, perhaps lost forever. Price had called in the new Intel during Phoenix's insertion into Jerusalem. According to the files, a weapons dump from Fortress Arms existed in the catacombs east of the Mosque el-Aksa. The original Solomon's Stables had been used in times of war to defend the Old City. The new addition to the catacombs had been built during the Six-Day War, then abandoned after the uneasy peace treaties had been agreed upon. After further investigation of the site, Kurtzman and his people determined that the catacombs had never been used since.

Reaching the archaeological excavations west of Haram esh-Sherif, Katz turned his steps toward the Chain Gate. He walked past a butcher's shop where eight disembodied sheep heads gazed through the window in eternal puzzlement.

"I hope that butcher's shop isn't an omen," Manning stated.

"Do you feel like a lamb being led to slaughter?"

"No, but I do hope this thing doesn't get out of hand. Besides the Muslim section being pissed-off at us, the Israelis aren't going to be any too thrilled, either."

Passing through the Chain Gate, Katz set foot into the Temple Mount sanctuary and immediately felt uneasy. That had been the mood every time he'd entered Haram esh-Sherif, although the area was held sacred by all three of Jerusalem's major religions. The literal cornerstone of the Islamic faith was contained within the walls of Haram esh-Sherif.

Although Temple Mount was identified as Abraham's altar, the Muslims believed Mohammed had crossed to the point during the middle of the night while riding a miraculous beast and accompanied by a band of angels.

Katz knew his crew of warriors were no angels, but they were fighting on the side of right. Since their arrival in Jerusalem, they'd already seen signs of the war that had started anew between the Israelis and the Palestinians. He didn't know for sure how many deaths had been claimed by either side, but the images of the white sheet-covered bodies being taken from the skirmish area on litters would be in his mind for a long time.

He tapped the transmit button on the headset. "Calvin."

"Go."

"Our path?"

"You're clear, and I've got your back door."

The Dome of the Rock was directly in front of Katz. Brilliantly colored panels, the gold dome and bands of phrases from the Koran around the octagonal walls made it the most beautiful place of worship in Jerusalem. Black-and-gold mosaics and stained-glass windows gave it a soft appearance, negating the harsh lines of the structure.

Dressed in tourist casualness, Rafael Encizo stood at the top of the steps at Katz's approach. He carried a worn and scuffed satchel the color of old caramel. As Katz and Manning passed, he fell into a loose rear guard.

A group of smaller Islamic buildings surrounded the Dome of the Rock, including the Dome of the Chain, a reduced version of Haram esh-Sherif's centerpiece. Down by the stairs and arches to the Mosque el-Aksa, people of the Islamic faith had gathered by the Mimber of Kadi Burhan ed-Din. The summer pulpit was going to feature a speaker later, protesting the newest peace treaty between Israel and the Palestinians.

Farther down the steps, Katz found the small building he was looking for. The structure was hardly big enough to hold two rooms and was made of stone and polished dark woods.

The special PA system that had been set up for the speaker at the summer pulpit crackled to life. Immediately a crowd started to drift toward the area and ignored the Phoenix Force members.

"They're on time," Manning growled.

"So are we," Katz said as he strode toward the front door. He riffled through the faces he'd memorized from the files Kurtzman had sent by computer, then unzipped the pocket at the bottom of the rucksack and palmed the SIG-Sauer P-226 he'd concealed there. He passed through the door and into the dark, cool interior of the building.

A hawk-nosed man in a robe and *ghutra* stood behind a small, ornate counter. Many pamphlets in different colors, all bearing flowing Arabic script, were arranged neatly across the countertop. His eyes were cold as he smiled. "Can I help you?" he asked in English.

Katz spoke in Arabic to make sure he was understood the first time. "Don't move." He lifted the SIG-Sauer into view.

"Who are you?"

"Someone who knows the Bloody Wind is only a refuge for terrorists and murderers." Katz waved the barrel of the gun. "Raise your hands and turn around."

The man acted as if he were going to comply, then spun and reached under the countertop. With a wild cry, he launched himself across the counter, scattering pamphlets, a curved dagger in his fist.

Katz moved fluidly to one side and raised his prosthesis in an open backhand slap. The blow landed with a meaty thwack and knocked the guy to the floor. The terrorist tried to get to his feet, but before he could, the Israeli met him with a spinning savate kick that stretched him out unconscious against a low-slung chair.

Encizo, an H&K MP-5 SD-3 up and ready, took a position at the doorway leading to the only other room. "Clear," he said tersely.

Katz nodded. "You have the point." He tapped the headset. "David."

"Go, mate."

"We've encountered some resistance."

The motorbike sounded throaty and strong over the frequency. "From the looks of things, you haven't managed to draw any attention. When you need me, I'll be there."

Katz gestured to Manning, stationing the big Canadian at the door.

"You're still clear from here also," James cut in over the channel. "Everyone's listening to the speaker or doing their own thing."

Satisfied that the terrorist's yell hadn't alerted anyone outside the building, Katz turned his attention to the inside of the structure.

The second room was smaller than the first and apparently used for informal entertainment. A water dispenser sat in one corner by a sofa and a small bookshelf holding little more than a dozen volumes. All the books were on the topic of Islam.

Eyes flicking about quickly, Katz concerned himself with the two walls at the far side of the room. Stained-glass windows decorated the other two. He pushed the SIG-Sauer into his belt at the back of his waistband and took a small stiletto from his ankle. Using the slim blade, he pried into the spaces were the walls met the ceiling.

"Nothing here," Encizo announced as he pushed himself up from a thorough survey under the couch.

The stiletto blade suddenly fell through a crack midway through the second wall. Katz pulled it back, feeling the draft of cool air ghosting through the space. "I found it. There must be a release lever somewhere."

"The purloined letter," Encizo said.

Katz looked at him.

"Did you notice any power lines to any of these small buildings?" the Cuban asked.

"No."

Encizo pointed. "Then why would they need a light switch?"

Katz glanced at the ivory-colored plate and toggle on the wall by the door, just where a switch would be on most rooms. "I guess they supposed most of the people who might investigate them would overlook that."

"I grew up without electricity," Encizo said. "I can still remember when light switches were a novelty."

Katz drew his pistol. "Try it." He turned to face the wall with the concealed door.

The switch clicked, but nothing happened. Undaunted, Encizo removed the Leatherman Multi-Tool from its pouch on his belt and used the screwdriver attachment to remove the switch plate. Inside the housing was another switch. He tripped it.

With a slight creaking, a three-by-four foot section of the wall swung away. A narrow stairway picked up some of the light coming through the windows on the twisting stone steps as it plunged downward.

Katz took the lead, letting the SIG-Sauer guide him.

"Who is there?" a sharp voice demanded in Arabic.

Leaning against the stone wall, Katz used his peripheral vision to pick up movement to his right. He tracked it with the pistol just as an AK-47-wielding terrorist stepped forward. The SIG-Sauer whispered and recoiled in his palm as he fired three quick rounds. All the bullets took the man in the face, but only one of them punched through, dragging sparks from the cut surface of the stone wall.

As the dead man fell away, the orange wavering glow of an oil lantern suddenly increased and threw out a bubble of light that filled the inside of the room. Four men dived away from a small folding table, clawing for their weapons.

Katz pushed himself to the side of the spiraling staircase, dropping the last few feet to the ground. Automatically targeting the nearest terrorist, he squeezed the trigger from point-blank range just as the hardman got off one round.

Katz felt as if he'd been hit in the rib cage by a sledgehammer. Air left his lungs in a sudden expulsion. Instead of giving in to the blinding pain, he focused on the terrorists and raised his weapon.

Without warning, the three remaining Bloody Wind terrorists started jerking in an uncoordinated dance. Cards flew from the folding table, then it buckled as one of the legs was shot away. The wooden crates filling the back of the underground vault splintered in places, but kept the subsonic 9 mm rounds from ricocheting. The lantern, hanging from a peg set into the wall, shattered and leaked a puddle of flames down the stone face and pooled on the floor.

"Katz," Encizo called out. The Cuban ejected the empty magazine from the submachine gun, then fitted a fresh clip immediately.

"I'm okay." The Israeli stood and rubbed his elbow over the painful area. The ballistic T-shirt under his clothing had stopped the bullet and the blunt trauma from the impact, but the force had still been impressive. The hot leaden mass fell from inside his shirt and hit the floor.

He tapped the transmit button. "Calvin?"

"We're secure."

Encizo moved forward and checked the bodies. He didn't bother to handcuff any of them.

Walking to the nearest wooden crate, Katz leathered the SIG-Sauer, then slipped a bayonet from one of the dead men's AK-47s. He slid the blade under the crate lid and shoved, ignoring the burning pain that wrapped around his rib cage. The nails shrieked as they turned loose. Inside, neatly stacked in foam pellets, was a brace of M-16s, looking and smelling freshly oiled.

Katz radioed Manning and asked him to join them. Encizo took the position up top.

As the demolitions expert for the team, the big Canadian was the only logical choice to dispose of the munitions in the safest manner possible. Located in Temple Mount, the Bloody Wind storehouse would have been offlimits to Israeli investigators, and a Mossad covert force would have guaranteed bloodshed. Even intervention by the Palestinians would have been heavy-handed, if they acted at all. Katz had seen no recourse but for a surgical strike by his team.

Manning slapped the walls experimentally. "I've seen the geographics of this area," he said as he shrugged out of his rucksack. "These walls are solid. They can withstand an implosion of the sort needed to nuke the weapons and leave everything standing. But I'm going to need an oxygen supply to feed the FAE."

Shrugging out of his own rucksack, Katz began taking out the compressed cans of fuel air explosive they'd brought along for the munitions work. What the explosion didn't render inoperative, the FAE would melt into slag. "What do you suggest?"

Manning pointed at the ceiling. "Near as I can figure it, that's the back wall of the building. Step it off and see if you agree."

Katz took the measurements with a practiced eye, then nodded. "I'd say that's about right." A packet of papers caught his attention and he picked them up. Some of the sheets were maps. He shoved them in his jacket pocket.

The Canadian continued to take gear out of his bag, including a battery-powered drill. "I can place some shaped charges in the ceiling and blow a hole through it a few seconds before I detonate the main load. There should be enough oxygen coming in then to fuel the FAE."

"Get it done."

Working quickly, Manning slipped on a pair of goggles and used the drill on the ceiling.

Katz set up a wide-beamed electric lantern and stepped back. Stone dust drifted down from the holes Manning drilled, and danced in the field of harsh, yellow light.

"Yakov," James radioed.

"Go." Katz had trouble hearing over the bite of the drill. He finished setting up the FAE canisters the way Manning had instructed, wiring them all into a remote-control detonator.

"We got trouble. I just picked up a couple Bloody Wind terrorists Aaron and Barb were able to ID, and they're headed your way."

"Affirmative." Katz looked at Manning. "You heard?"

"Yeah." Manning put the drill away and started packing C-4 plastique into the three holes he'd drilled, smashing the explosive deep with his thumb, then using a wooden dowel. "Be done in just a minute with this. You ready there?"

"Yes."

The big Canadian added detonators, plugging them in carefully.

Encizo broke into the com link. "They're definitely headed this way. How do you want to handle this?"

"I'm on my way." Katz navigated the stairs, removing an Uzi from his nearly depleted rucksack. Back in the first room, he waved Encizo into the corner and gazed through the door as five men approached the entrance. He kept the Uzi hidden behind the counter.

The lead man ducked through the door, then stopped quick enough that the guy following him almost ran him over. He was thin and rangy like a wolf, with a thick mustache and beard. Pale gray eyes, the right one half hooded by scar tissue from an encounter with a blade in years past, locked solidly on Katz's.

"Who are you?" the man demanded in Arabic. "And where is Mahmud?"

"Mahmud's indisposed," Katz replied. "And I'm here to put the Bloody Wind out of business."

Katz cut loose with a deadly figure eight, the silenced burst of rounds catching two of the terrorists and knocking them backward. A metallic globe came bouncing into the room, ricocheted from the counter and sat spinning on the floor.

"Grenade!" Encizo yelled.

"Move!" Katz ordered. He scrambled on top of the counter, balanced himself on his prosthesis as a bullet took off the last two fingers and dived for the nearby stained-glass window nearest him, Manning and Encizo at his heels.

The glass shattered as he went through with his arm held protectively across his face. Autofire tracked across the window and plucked more glass fragments free of the frame. Unable to land on his feet, worried that he might impede Manning's escape, he rolled to the side, cradling the Uzi inside his arms. He came to a halt on his right foot and left knee just as the grenade exploded.

The vibrant thunderclap spread throughout Haram esh-Sherif. At the summer pulpit, the crowd ran for cover with practiced ease.

The rolling crack of Calvin James's M-21 Beretta sniper rifle rang out, and one of the terrorists near the building suddenly pitched forward, then lay still on the stones.

"You got more on their way," the ex-SEAL warned. "Coming in at three o'clock."

Glancing to his right, Katz saw the small phalanx of Bloody Wind gunners closing in on him from forty meters away, shoving their way through the crowd on the walkways. When he was sure of the fire zone, he unleashed a firestorm of 9 mm rounds on full-auto. At least two more rounds smashed painfully into his ballistic T-shirt.

Four of the terrorists went down; the rest scattered.

As he ejected the empty magazine, Katz scoped the terrain for the two other Phoenix Force warriors directly involved in the engagement. Manning had taken up a position at the side of another small building. There was no sign of Encizo. The Israeli tapped the headset button. "Rafael."

"Still standing, amigo."

"Are you able to move?"

"Not at the moment. I'm pinned down."

"I'm on it, Katz," James radioed.

The crashing din of gunfire rolled and thundered in the enclosed space of Haram esh-Sherif. Even the parapets seemed to be vibrating in response.

"Gary," the Israeli called out.

"Yeah."

"Let's get it done and be on our way before things get any more complicated."

"Right." Manning lifted the detonator and keyed in the codes he'd preset.

A terrorist tried to break cover and approach Katz's position. Using an economical triburst, the Israeli stitched the man across the chest and sent him spinning away.

Then the first explosion trembled through the ground. A glance at the back of the building showed a crater the size of a manhole cover suddenly implode less than a meter behind the back wall. Instead of rock being forcibly blown out of the hole, it seemed to crack, then fall back on itself, removing the danger of flying debris injuring innocents.

"Magic," Manning said. He depressed the second code.

Another rumble shook the immediate vicinity, and tongues of white-hot flames stabbed through the hole. Twisting black streamers of smoke followed, launching themselves at the blue sky like hungry snakes.

"Let's go," Katz said, taking the lead. Manning followed, pausing only to unleash a burst from the H&K MP-5 that took down two terrorists.

The Israeli skirted close to the building at a jog, managing to hang the Uzi from a Whip-it sling over his shoulder. He palmed two smoke grenades as he passed the hole where the FAE still burned. The heat washed over him, assuring him that there wouldn't be anything salvageable from the hoard of weapons.

Rounding the corner, Katz saw Encizo pinned down behind a stone pillar supporting an ornate arch. The Israeli slipped the pins on the smoke grenades and hurled the canisters toward the Cuban. Just as they exploded, Katz lifted the Uzi and fired from the point, throwing enough lead at a trio of terrorists trying to flank Encizo to send them scurrying for cover.

Dense red smoke, spreading like blood in water, drifted into the still air in front of the trapped Phoenix Force warrior. Wheeling suddenly to take advantage of the brief cover, Encizo ran to join Katz and Manning. He had to leap two bodies with head wounds that were mute testimony to James's skill with the sniper rifle.

Two screaming terrorists charged through the smokescreen with their guns blazing. Dropping to one knee, Manning swept them away with a blistering 9 mm figure eight.

Tapping his headset transmit button, Katz called for McCarter.

"Go, mate."

"Which way?" There were five entrances to Haram esh-Sherif, counting the two gates and three streets.

"The Chain Gate's been bloody well blocked by Israeli soldiers," McCarter replied. "And you can bet the Golden Gate will be, too."

Katz flicked through the mental map he'd made of the area while racing in a loop around the outskirts of Haram esh-Sherif. "Let's make for Antonia, then. That will give us options from that point."

"Agreed, mate. I'll see you there."

The Dome of the Chain was to Katz's left. A backward glance showed him the robed figures of the Bloody Wind falling into their backtrail, roughly pushing aside the frightened people frozen in their tracks. Two of the lead terrorists suddenly went slack and fell to the ground, bringing down two more of their comrades. The other gunners ran for cover. Katz recognized the stunning authority of the Beretta M-21 sniper rifle.

He thumbed the headset. "Calvin?"

"I copied," James said confidently. "Just taking care of your lead. Don't worry. When you guys reach Antonia, you won't be waiting on me."

Katz concentrated on running. He made the Uzi visible, warning off whatever interference might have been offered.

James was waiting for them by the exit leading out to Antonia Street. The ex-SEAL looked winded, but his grip on his rifle was calm and sure.

Without breaking stride, Katz followed Antonia long enough to find a series of alleys that would take him to Lion Gate. He informed McCarter of the decision by radio, then heard the rumble of the motorbike somewhere behind them.

They sprinted through an alley filled with men hawking vegetables, poultry and lambs, where children sat in groups and played games, not really interested in four men rushing past. In Jerusalem, it wasn't uncommon to see someone fleeing for his life.

"Dump the heavy artillery," Katz instructed as they neared Lion Gate. He wiped down the Uzi and dropped it in a garbage bin. He was just getting his second wind when they raced through the gate. Beyond it, Jericho Road held a fair amount of traffic. He kept the SIG-Sauer in his waistband.

"Here," James called out. He pointed to a light blue Ford van parked in a cul-de-sac.

Katz changed directions as a huge flatbed truck with a canvas awning pulled off Jericho Road onto Via Doloroad, approaching them. Through the dust-encrusted, bug-spattered windshield, the Israeli saw three men. Two of them had assault weapons visible.

He hit the transmit button on the headset as James and Encizo worked at breaking into the van. "David."

"I see them, mate. You people hold tight."

The man seated next to the flatbed driver threw a hand out, pointing at Katz. The man in the passenger seat scrambled to lean out the window and bring his weapon to bear. A line of bullets chipped splinters from the bricks by Katz's face.

Then the fierce blat of a motorbike engine washed over the straining sounds of the truck's transmission. David McCarter flashed by and dropped a H&K 33E assault rifle onto the motorbike's handlebars. Speeding toward the huge truck, McCarter resembled a knight from his native country's distant past taking on a lumbering dragon. The full-throated blast of the assault rifle opened up, taking out the flatbed's front tires.

The truck turned sideways in the road, coming up on two tires and nearly toppling over. Ground troops in the back ripped the canvas away from the steel rib cage, revealing more than a dozen more gunners in the back.

With a deft hand, McCarter skated around the truck, riding up on the sidewalk for a moment and dodging two pushcarts stocked with foodstuffs. The pushcart owners took refuge in the recessed door of a candle shop.

The gunners in the rear of the flatbed took aim at the Briton. Snarling the gears, the truck driver struggled to get it turned around.

Katz and Manning leveled their pistols and fired as quickly as they could, buying their teammate some respite.

Coolly, thirty meters from the rocking flatbed, Mc-Carter dropped his boot and brought the motorbike around in a tight 180-degree turn. He threw his leg over the motorbike, reached for his vest pocket and brought out a fat cigar-shaped device that he fitted to the end of the H&K 33E with practiced ease.

As Katz changed magazines, he watched McCarter adjust the FN Bullet-Through rifle grenade's plastic flip-up foresight, then telescope the grenade's body to finish prepping it. The Briton shouldered his weapon and fired almost immediately. The tremendous recoil shoved him back.

Activated by the gases following the fired round, the grenade whooshed toward the flatbed and struck the back of the cab. The antipersonnel high-explosive warhead scythed through the terrorists like a twister through a field of scarecrows. The truck kept rolling, the rear window warped and the man sitting in the middle in the cab was nearly decapitated. McCarter's second grenade was an antivehicle charge. He punched it into the side of the truck, which rocked violently. Gasoline pooled under the vehicle, then caught fire, spiraling up in blue and yellow vines.

"Katz," James yelled. "We're mobile."

The Israeli pulled back to the van and took the passenger seat. Encizo and Manning crowded into the rear.

Pulling hard on the wheel, James steered the van out into the street and swerved around the burning flatbed. The few terrorists that had survived McCarter's attack were disoriented and in no shape to continue the fight.

Ahead of them, McCarter had remounted his mechanical steed and offered them a salute and a smile. "Where to now, Katz?"

"The safehouse." From inside his shirt, Katz slipped the papers he'd recovered from the Bloody Wind site and started to leaf through them. One of the bullets that had been stopped by the ballistic T-shirt had cored through the folded papers, leaving a gaping hole. Still, there was no denying the map that he found in the middle of them. It was of the hotels where the peace conferences between the Palestinians and Israel had been taking place. And there was a road map of the route Katz knew through Secret Service records that the President would be taking in from the airport.

"Something?" Encizo asked from the seat behind him.

Katz passed the papers back as James made a right-hand turn onto Jericho Road and merged with the traffic. "There's no mistaking their target," the Israeli said gruffly.

"Yeah, but this marks only the Bloody Wind's planned attempt." The Cuban looked up at him. "It doesn't say anything about what other groups are headed by a Huntsman who might be coordinating the effort."

Katz nodded, remembering how their first action in Jerusalem had resulted in innocent blood being spilled. "Until we know more, we're compelled to assume the President's going to be running a gauntlet from the time he steps off Air Force One."

James glanced at his watch. "That's only hours away."

"We'll have to make every moment count," Katz said.

10

Stony Man Farm

Barbara Price and Mack Bolan stood in one of the bed-room/holding cells on the top floor of the Farm's main house, staring through one-way glass at the woman held in an office chair by restraining straps. Bolan leaned forward and turned up the microphone pickup on the audio equipment.

A blank expression filled the auburn-haired woman's face. Her eyes were rolled up until almost only the blood-shot whites showed. She wore a tan coverall and soft gray slippers. Sterile, white bandages on the insides of both elbows stood out even against the pale of her skin, testifying to the number of shots and blood tests she'd been given.

"Do you know her name?" Bolan asked.

"Giselle Harte." Price handed over a slim manila file folder. "It's pretty much in there."

Glancing through the file, the warrior got a sense of the woman. Like the other Huntsman alters, Harte had once been in law enforcement. She'd served her time in the Seattle PD and left under a cloud of suspicion, eventually ending up with the private-investigation agency where she'd won her trip to Monte Carlo.

"She's lost a lot of years," Bolan commented when he put the file away.

"From what we've seen, she was one of the longest under. It's going to leave scars."

On the other side of the glass, Dr. Vivian Brookshaus entered the room. Through the doorway, a grim-faced blacksuit could be seen standing guard in the hallway.

"Can you track her back?" Bolan asked.

"Not for the last four years. Before that we can verify that she worked in a shipping office in Houston for the Port Authority under the name of Felicia Huddleston. As Cherie Lee Davis, she worked as a magician's helper at an amusement park in Orlando. She left fingerprints at the Port Authority records that matched up to the ones Aaron sent out, and she had an outstanding warrant for her arrest in Orlando for a DUI."

"They printed her there?"

"Yeah."

"Did you get a look at the files?"

"Akira ripped off copies. I went over them. So did Brookshaus."

"Was the DUI charge legit?"

Price crossed her arms over her breasts. "She was definitely under the influence of something, but none of the blood tests or the breathalyzer could figure out what. Brookshaus thinks she was trying to come out from under the programming and got jammed up."

"What happened?"

"She disappeared that night. Never went back to her job or her apartment. Brookshaus thinks she's been conditioned to call a control person when she starts feeling the split. That person resets the conditioning with certain passwords. That's standard operating procedure for people suffering from multiple personalities."

Brookshaus took a chair from a small desk that had been set up in the room, then rolled it to a stop in front of her patient. Her white lab coat was open, and she had the sleeves rolled up. She leaned in close to Harte and spoke in a soft, hypnotic voice. "I want to speak to Giselle."

"There's no one here by that name," Harte said in harsh tones. "I am the Huntsman. I'm eternal."

"Dr. Brookshaus explained to me that the Huntsman personality is the glue that binds the rest of the mosaic together," Price said. "It's also wrapped around the part of the woman that's still Giselle Harte. In order to restore the core personality, that of Harte, she has to back the Huntsman alter off."

"How?"

"The Huntsman alter is false. Although it believes itself to be real, there are things it can't know about the real Alexander De Moray. Brookshaus is going to try to pull at the fabric of lies until it collapses. With all the drugs and the counterconditioning she's done, as well as the information we have now on De Moray, she believes she can reach Harte and bring her to the surface."

"Will she stay in control?" Bolan tried to imagine what might be going on in the woman's head but couldn't. His world had been filled forever with black and white, good and evil, and a sure knowledge of himself no matter what circumstances he might be in. It was hard to fathom being lost in his own mind.

"Brookshaus thinks so. She learned a lot from the other alters that we've encountered."

In the other room, the doctor held up a key case with one of the Vietnamese bottlecaps mounted on it. "Tell me about this," Brookshaus suggested.

Harte laughed, harsh and raucous. Her eyes focused on the key case for an instant, then rolled back up in her head. "That's my good-luck charm."

"Where did you get it?"

"Khe Sahn, lady. Ever hear of it?"

"It was a battle in Vietnam."

"No shit."

"You were there?"

"Me and a lot of other guys."

"Guys?"

"Yeah."

"Do you know what you look like?"

"What kind of question is that?"

Brookshaus spoke intently. "It's just a question. Why are you so defensive?"

"I'm not defensive."

The words sounded definite and final, but Bolan could tell from the tight way the woman held herself that she was really very insecure with the line of questioning.

Brookshaus held up the key case again. "Tell me about the bottlecap."

"It's a keepsake."

"Why?"

"Because maybe it kept me alive."

"What makes you think that?"

"You had to be there."

"Take me there." Brookshaus's voice was almost a whisper now.

For a moment Bolan didn't think the woman was going to speak.

"She's accessing the implanted memories," Price stated. "The Huntsman alter is a specific mode of behavior that's been layered in. Basically there's another personality who's in charge of the false records, according to what I understand from Brookshaus. The Huntsman alter has to go to the records-keeper to reference things from the perceived past."

"She did this with the other alters?" Price nodded.

"It was in Khe Sahn," the woman said in a halting voice. "Right before the big push from Charlie."

Bolan remembered those days. They'd been nothing short of hellish, and death had swept across several battlefields.

"I was on patrol, just retired from point and hanging with the main body of my unit. If you're on point long enough, you don't like pulling back out of that position. You don't trust anyone else to really take care of the squad. But I had a green second looie calling the moves, and Sergeant Connors hadn't been able to really tell this guy how things were out in the jungle, the way he did with our last CO. We were a fucking accident waiting to happen. And it did." Giselle Harte stopped talking. Perspiration trickled down her face.

"Go on," Brookshaus directed. "You're safe here with me. Take a deep breath and let yourself feel the room around you."

Harte released a long exhalation.

"Now," Brookshaus said, "go back. Your patrol was attacked."

"They came out of nowhere," Harte went on. "Like goddamn ghosts. Before I knew it, bullets were flying everywhere, and grenades were popping as quick as party favors. Sergeant Connors went down with half his head blown away. Our radio guy was next. We never had a chance. In less than a minute, eighty percent of the squad was FUBAR."

Bolan knew the term. The psychologist didn't and asked for clarification.

"Fucked up beyond all repair," Harte said. "Ready for body bags."

"Where were you?" Brookshaus asked.

"I was hit." The woman touched her chest near the sternum. "Two rounds in my upper chest. Thank God they both missed my lungs. Another round through my left thigh. I dropped and went into shock, lying on my stomach and listening to the gunfire."

"Were you scared?"

"No."

"Why?"

"I knew I wasn't going to die."

"How did you know?"

"Because I can't die," Harte said confidently. "I come back. The Huntsman is eternal."

"The real De Moray would have been afraid," Bolan said. "Every soldier in battle is afraid at one time or another."

Price nodded. "That's where Brookshaus thinks she can start breaking down the controlling alter. Giselle Harte, wherever she is inside that body, is smart enough to know that fear is a natural thing, and that anyone can be killed. Brookshaus thinks Harte might be the best subject available to break the programming. The episode in Orlando suggests that the core personality was trying to break free of the alter. And some of the answers to questions in an earlier session make her think the same thing. We should know soon."

Brookshaus held up the key case. "Tell me about the bottlecap."

"It was on the ground," Harte said. "Only a few inches from my face. I knew I was bleeding pretty bad, but I also knew I couldn't move."

"Why?"

"Because they would kill me."

"How?"

"A bullet through the head. They had guys walking through the bodies with pistols, finishing up anyone who was still alive. If I'd moved, they would have killed me."

"You're sure."

"Hell, yes."

"But you told me you couldn't be killed."

"I can't be."

Brookshaus made her voice more patient. "I'm confused. Were you afraid of being killed?"

"No. I can't be killed."

"I understand that. But, that day, if you'd moved they would have killed you."

"Yes."

"How? If you can't be killed, how could they have killed you?"

Price leaned toward the glass expectantly. "There's one of the flaws Brookshaus discovered. The bottlecap was used as a physical touchstone with the Huntsman alter. She thinks it was taken from a real emotion that originally came from De Moray. It's possible they taped a session with De Moray under deep hypnosis. They edited out the memory of fear, but left in the conflict about life or death."

"And overlaid it with the belief that the Huntsman could never be killed," Bolan stated.

"Yes, and it created a dichotomy."

Her back rigid and her eyes rolled up in her head, Harte was unresponsive.

"The bottlecap," Brookshaus reminded gently.

"It was on the ground," Harte said. "Pressed down into the trail. I was lying there, waiting for the bullet, listening to the men walk through my squad. The pistols fired sporadically. I couldn't run. Not with those wounds. So I laid there and concentrated on that bottlecap.''

"This bottlecap?"

"Yes. I focused everything I had on it, put myself outside my body until I was in control. At first I didn't even hear the helicopter gunships. I felt the guy step on my leg. I never even saw his face, but I knew he was about to pull the trigger. Then a door gunner opened up and blew him away. Charlie pulled up stakes and ran."

"And you lived?"

"Yes."

"When you thought you wouldn't."

"Yes."

"What about the bottlecap?"

"I closed my fist around it and passed out. When I came to in the base camp hospital, I still had it in my hand. They never even noticed it in surgery."

"So you've had it ever since."

"Yes."

"How do you explain being so sure you were going to die if you know you can't?"

Harte didn't answer.

"There's a part of you that's afraid of dying," Brookshaus said confidently.

There was a hesitation, then, "She's weak and afraid."

"Giselle?"

"Yes."

"You know about Giselle?"

A sneer settled over the woman's lips. "Yes. She didn't want to kill the target in Miami."

"Why?"

"Because he was a cop."

"Why would she care?"

"She was a cop."

Brookshaus leaned back but remained intently focused on her patient.

On the other side of the glass, Bolan felt the tension inside the room settling over him. He found himself breathing more shallowly and shifted his shoulders to loosen the weight he hadn't known he was holding. He felt anxious to do something, but there was nothing to do at the moment. Hayden Thone had seemed to vanish from the face of the earth, and as yet there wasn't a lead about where to begin to look. The terrorist attacks around the globe had continued to escalate, but responding to any one of them would have been a waste of time. The Huntsman program was the driving force behind the attacks, and Giselle Harte might have the key to that.

"How much do you know about Harte?" Brookshaus asked.

"She's weak."

"And you're not."

"No."

"Do you know what she looks like?"

"Yes."

"Where have you seen her?"

"In my head." Harte's eyes closed. "I don't want to talk about that bitch."

Brookshaus ignored the protest. "You've seen her in your head?"

"I'm not going to talk about this."

"Don't. But you're going to think about it, aren't you? You've been thinking about Giselle Harte for a long time. And you've seen her in more places than just inside your head. Haven't you?"

"Go away."

"You've seen her in the mirror, haven't you?"

"No."

"Every time you look at a mirror to comb your hair. Every time you pass by a reflective surface, you see her."

"No."

"That's because you're in Giselle Harte's body," Brookshaus said. "You're a figment of someone's sick imagination. A pale copy of a very warped original."

"You're lying!" The tone was vehement. The woman lunged against the restraints, trying to get to her tormentor.

Suddenly wan and tense, Brookshaus leaned back in her chair slightly. "I want you to release Giselle Harte."

"No!"

"Tell me again about Vietnam." Brookhaus shifted directions.

The woman settled down, but held a wary posture. "What do you want to know?"

"I want to know the name of the man lying next to you when you were on that trail."

"I don't know."

"Tell me the name of the man next to him."

"I don't know." Uncertainty colored the voice and worry etched into the woman's features.

"What was the lieutenant's name?"

"Thornton."

"What was his first name?"

"I don't know."

"Wouldn't the real Alexander De Moray know?"

"I am real."

"Then tell me the lieutenant's first name."

"I can't. I don't remember. Randy." Desperation tainted the words.

Price was quiet when she spoke. "Either the Huntsman alter will fade, or she'll go catatonic. But we need whatever information she may possess."

"The lieutenant's name," Brookshaus said with calm authority, "was Harvey."

"I remember."

"Do you?"

"Yes."

"I don't believe you."

Harte shook her head. Perspiration ran in beads down her face, staining her coverall. "It doesn't matter."

"When did you join the military?" Brookshaus asked.

"July 12."

"Why?"

"I don't understand."

"It's a simple question. Why did you join the military?"

"I don't know."

"Don't you think you should?"

"Stop!"

"Tell me about the bottlecap."

"What do you want to know?" Harte's eyelids were flickering.

"What did it feel like?"

"I don't understand."

"What did the bottlecap feel like?"

"Hard. It was hard."

"Cold or hot?"

"I don't know."

"You should. That bottlecap saved your life. You should know everything there is to know about that piece of metal."

"I do know."

"What did the jungle smell like that day?"

"I don't know."

"You were lying on top of it. Put yourself back there. Feel the weight of the equipment."

"I can't."

"Were your clothes wet? It was hot that day."

"I don't know."

Brookshaus's voice sharpened. "The real Alexander De Moray would know. They made you, cobbled you together from his memories filtered through years of experiences, and tied them all together with drugs, hypnosis and conditioning. Don't you remember that?"

"It didn't happen!"

"Sure it did. You've got to remember the shots, the voices talking to you all the time, telling you about this person you were going to become. Do you remember the lights? Where did they keep you?"

"In a small room."

"Were there any windows?"

"No."

"Were there a lot of lights?"

"All the time. I couldn't escape them." Harte's voice had become a hoarse whisper.

"They didn't let you sleep."

"Not much. I was never rested. Shocks." She held herself. "They shocked me all the time. I had to pay attention. The man next to me…they weren't watching him and he slit his wrists with a razor one of the attendants left after shaving him. He bled all over his sheets. They took him away."

"Where were you? What city?"

Harte's voice changed again, becoming more coarse. "You're trying to trick me. None of that ever happened."

"They say you took graft money in Seattle."

"That's a lie!"

"Your partner was taking graft, and you knew it. Why didn't you turn him in?"

Bolan watched the struggle showing on the woman's face, knowing it was only a small part of what was going on in her mind. He wished that they had more time to be gentle with her, but it wasn't possible. Too many people were dying.

"Because he was my partner," Harte answered.

"That made people think you were in with him."

"I know."

"Did you take money?"

"No."

Brookshaus made her voice accusing. "You took the money."

"No!" Harte's head whipped back and forth.

"You betrayed your badge and your friends. You sold them out."

"No, damn it! I never took anything! I just protected my partner!" The woman was seized by an uncontrollable fit of crying. Tears ran down her face as her shoulders were racked by sobs. Long minutes passed.

"Who are you?" Brookshaus asked gently.

The woman lifted her head. She looked frightened and alone. "Giselle Harte. Would you please tell me where I am?"

"Sure, but we need to talk a little more first. Would you like something to drink?"

"Yes."

Brookshaus left the room. Behind her, Harte tried to raise her arms but couldn't. She sat there quietly, tears streaming down her face as she stared at the one-way glass.

"She knows we're here," Price said.

"I know." Bolan turned away. "I need to talk to her as soon as I can."

Price nodded, obviously affected by the woman's discomfort and confusion.

Gently the Executioner took Price in his arms and held her tight. "Barb, you and I both know that justice isn't always possible. Cannibals don't know justice. Sometimes vengeance is the best that you can offer. I knew that when I picked up the gun in Pittsfield. And as long as I can deal out revenge for the vulnerable innocents that can't deal it out for themselves, I will." He smoothed the mission controller's hair as he stared at the vulnerable innocent in the other room.

11

Miami, Florida

"So where's your boy?" George Cosgrove demanded. He stood in the center of the hotel lobby amid the white chalk marks left by the crime-scene unit. He waved at the empty shadows where dead men had lain only moments ago. "An impressive body count like this, I figure he'd been calling you up wanting a pat on the head."

Brognola chewed on his cigar but didn't say anything. He'd been wondering when Cosgrove would blow. Hours had passed since the attempt on his life.

Uniformed officers from the Miami PD still stalked the halls of the hotel, interviewing guests. The descriptions of the Executioner were amazingly incongruent. The Miami detectives working the case weren't happy to be rubbing shoulders with so many federal and international cops. Advice and criticism flew faster and faster as the investigation dragged on. "Too goddamn many chiefs and not enough Indians," one of the uniforms protested from the desk.

The media were still poised outside the lobby doors, the street littered with vans and cars. The Miami PD's job was made even harder because a media blackout had been dropped over the investigation to protect the identities of the international task force. It was possible they would become targets as well.

"It's fucking amazing how he managed to kill them all," Cosgrove said, "then run off with the only surviving witness."

"Where is this guy and the woman he's supposed to have with him?" Harry Wu asked.

Brognola shook his head. "I can't say." The Stony Man Farm hardsite had to be protected no matter what else happened. He'd agreed to that when he took over the job, even if he hadn't believed that secrecy was one of the Farm's chief weapons in its arsenal.

"Can't or won't?" Michael Ferris demanded.

"Same difference."

"Terrific."

Brognola knew at the moment he didn't have a friend in the room.

"Did you call this guy in?" Cosgrove asked.

"No."

"So somebody's looking out for your interests. Do they deduct that out of what they pay you, or is that a fringe benefit?"

Brognola swept the room with a glance, finding nothing but hard-eyed interest looking back at him. The crime-scene investigation team had cleared him with the detectives almost twenty minutes ago. He figured it was time to go.

He took his cigar out of his mouth and threw it toward one of the burnished copper freestanding ashtrays near the door. The cigar hit the white sand, then skidded over the top, scattering sand in its wake. "You can look at this any way you want to, but I'm not going to stand here and be insulted. We're on the same side. If you don't want to believe that, tough shit."

Cosgrove took a threatening step forward, maintaining his distance to a degree. Evidently he hadn't forgotten that his attempt at getting physical the previous day hadn't gone over well. He pointed at the big Fed with a thick forefinger as he spoke. "You're dirty, Brognola, and I'm the guy who's going to prove it. And when I do, I'm going to take you in myself."

Gazing coolly over the callused finger, Brognola said, "You're going to look damn funny with that finger shoved up your ass." He pushed past the man and kept his head held up. It wasn't the first time he'd been between a rock and a hard place.

Once on the street he felt better. He didn't try to keep his face covered. His name had already leaked out to the press, and they could dig up file photos from the morgue at their leisure. For the moment, though, he was living life under a microscope. The thing he hated most was that for a time he wouldn't be able to find out if Bolan had discovered anything from the woman Huntsman. He squared his shoulders and ignored the front line of reporters that rushed him. Hayden Thone's fortress of cards was falling down around him, and the thought gave Brognola some comfort.

STANDING IN THE HALLWAY on the second floor of the office building across from the hotel, Alexander De Moray watched Brognola's departure through a small pair of binoculars.

Once he lost sight of the Justice agent, he switched back to the lobby in time to watch the rest of the task force exit the building. He hummed to himself as he watched, a hot zydeco beat that reminded him of the French Quarter peep shows his uncle had taken him to when he was only fourteen.

He recognized the Treasury agent, Cosgrove, and he considered the interesting lines that had come up between the man and Brognola. It was easy to figure that Brognola was still a threat, connected somewhere along the way to the covert force dogging the Fortress Arms web spread around the globe. The misdirection about Brognola working the task force in Miami had cost time. He and Thone had both figured the Intel going into the covert force was coming from the task force people. But their surveillance of the international law-enforcement teams involved had netted nothing.

Still, it had given him an unexpected lever.

A door opened behind him, and he turned to face the CPA he'd bumped into earlier when taking up a position in the office building.

"Getting anything?" the accountant asked as he locked up his office. He was tan and balding, and De Moray figured the guy was off for an early-afternoon five-mile run.

De Moray smiled. "Be better if I knew how to read lips. I got a few pictures, though." He patted the camera with the telescopic lens hanging at his side.

"You and every other reporter in this town are covering those murders. For Christ's sake, this is Miami. This time tomorrow, there'll be two times as many."

"Yeah, but today I've got these to cover."

Tossing him a salute, the CPA took the stairs and headed down. His easy rhythm told De Moray he probably did a pretty fast five miles.

After waiting a couple extra minutes in case the guy forgot anything, the Cajun went to his office door, picked the lock with a rubber band and a paper clip and let himself inside. The office lacked frills but had an autographed baseball card of Pete Rose in a gilt frame on the wall. He studied the card as he sat behind the desk, picked up the phone and punched in Thone's number.

"Hello," the Fortress Arms CEO said.

"We missed on the Miami special," De Moray stated without preamble.

"I heard. What happened?"

"We also lost the gun."

"Dead?"

"Unfortunately, no." There was a pause, during which De Moray considered the framed baseball card.

"She wasn't very stable."

"I know. You should have used someone else."

"There wasn't anyone else."

A glance out the window showed De Moray that the news vehicles were starting to leave. "I think I've got another angle on the party at this end."

"I think I'd rather have you in Juarez. We haven't shut down the operation there."

"It would help to have this guy out of the way. From what I've seen today, he carries some heavy weight."

"How long would it take?"

"An hour. No more than two, probably."

"Okay. Get it done, then get down to Juarez. There're too many ties to that installation and other things I've kept hidden from public record that I can't afford to have turned up."

"Right."

"Let me know when you get there."

De Moray broke the connection and watched George Cosgrove get into an unmarked sedan double-parked in front of the hotel. He rested his chin on his knuckles as he yawned. He already had Cosgrove's hotel and room number through the earlier investigation Thone's teams had conducted. Only the timing remained to chance.

He stood to go. As an afterthought, he took the Pete Rose card. When he got back to New Orleans, his Uncle Remy would love to have it.

FOR THE PAST HOUR, Giselle Harte had unraveled a story of cold horror, detailing as well as she could the building where she and more than a dozen other people had been kept while being programmed with the Huntsman alters.

Mack Bolan sat on the other side of the long conference table in the War Room and watched the woman. He kept his feelings neutral, taking in her information the same way he'd have absorbed Intel from a recon scout who'd had a personal vision of hell. Her pain and suffering were apparent, but she didn't dwell on them.

She'd been aware only of the building where she'd been held for a few days, and memory of that was flawed. The one thing she'd remembered that was of value was the discovery of a handbill listing the Mission de Nuestra Señora de Guadalupe while she was being held in an RV, and that they'd crossed the Rio Grande on Highway 45.

Kurtzman sat at a computer console to one side of the room and tapped the keys rapidly. At the head of the table, Price finished up a quiet, short conversation with Carl Lyons over the telephone. Her face gave nothing away.

Dr. Vivian Brookshaus sat beside Harte, her look detached, but the pain in her eyes was apparent to Bolan. She stood and squeezed the woman's shoulder. "Would you like some coffee?"

"Yes. Two creams and a sugar." Harte took a sudden deep breath, then let it out slowly. Her eyes met Bolan's. "Does your file on me say anything about how I take my coffee?" She forced a brittle laugh. "It gets pretty weird when I start wondering whether I take my coffee that way or one of these other personalities does. Or if I even like coffee."

Bolan smoothed a hand over the manila file in front of him. "No."

Brookshaus walked to the coffee service at the side of the room and fixed the two coffees. "Giselle, to be frank and to leave the clinical talk behind for a while, you've been through a hell of a time emotionally for years. You can't expect to come to terms with it in a matter of hours. But it can be done, and I'll help you do it if you want me to."

Looking at her hands on the table in front of her, Harte continued methodically tearing apart a paper tissue she'd held.

Brookhaus handed her a foam cup. "You can be sure this is the way you take your coffee. You *are* yourself again. The only thing we need to do is incorporate those other memories back into your core personality and give you as much of those years back as we can."

"What if I don't want all those memories back?"

"Then we'll leave them out."

"It's that easy?"

Brookshaus sat down. "No. But I am good at what I do."

"Striker," Kurtzman called.

"Yeah?"

"I found the church." Tapping the keys more, Kurtzman brought up the room's wall screens. There was a splash of rainbow across all four screens, then they cleared as a picture took form.

The lines of the church were hard and well-defined, and filled out with adobe brick baked alabaster by an unforgiving sun. The overtones were definitely Spanish.

"Where?" Bolan asked, taking in as much of the flat land and red dirt around the mission as he could.

"Ciudad Juarez." Kurtzman leaned back in his wheelchair and studied the monitor in front of him that reflected the image in much smaller dimensions. "The Mission de Nuestra Señora de Guadalupe was built more than three hundred years ago and is a shrine to Mexico's patron saint. There's only the one."

"Does Fortress Arms own any property there?" the warrior asked.

Kurtzman shook his head. "Not that I could turn up. But I haven't gotten everything there is to know about the corporation yet. Hell, the financing on Fortress Arms during the change from Festung Armor is spread across half of Europe and through some of the Middle East. His list of backers include Libyan, Syrian and Iraqi interests. If knowledge of that had hit Wall Street, the company would never have become one of the Fortune 500 picks."

Shifting his attention to Harte, Bolan asked, "Does the church look familiar?"

She studied it quietly for a moment, then shrugged. "I don't know. I clearly remember the pamphlet, though."

"It's possible she was never there," Price pointed out as she put the phone away.

"What can you get on the rest of the city?" Bolan asked Kurtzman.

"Coming up." The keyboard clacked.

In response, the picture of the mission disappeared and was replaced by street scenes from Ciudad Juarez. For the next fifteen minutes Kurtzman provided a sparse, running commentary on the graphic interchange format package he'd lifted from a tourism data base in Dallas.

"I don't know. Some of it looks familiar, but I can't remember for sure."

"It could be some of her memories are tainted by the overlays that were going on at that time," Brookshaus said.

"Wait!" Harte pointed. "I know that fountain. Go back." Kurtzman tapped the keyboard and reversed the flow of pictures. "Go back a couple more. There."

The picture was of a park area, the yard a brilliant green. In the center was a large fountain with three huge carp leaping from the spigot of water that spewed upward.

"I've been there." Harte's brow furrowed in concentration, and she rubbed her temples as if she had a headache. "I'd almost gotten away once. I think. I remember coming to, like I'd just awakened. I was confused and scared. Before I could go very far, a guy with a mustache—maybe a beard—with the top of his left ear missing, grabbed me and gave me an injection." She held herself and talked more softly. "I screamed for help, but no one came. People were all around me talking, but I couldn't understand any of them. Then I don't remember anything else."

Bolan looked at Price.

"Your call," the mission controller said. "I don't have anything better to give you at the moment."

Turning over the possibilities open to him, Bolan said, "We go. Jack can fly us in as far as El Paso. After that, we're on our own. If you turn up something further regarding Thone, I'll have to make the jump from somewhere."

Price nodded.

"I'm going with you," Harte stated with quiet determination.

The warrior looked at the woman. "I don't know that you're ready for that."

"Giselle," Brookshaus said, turning to Harte, "you've just been through more than most people have to deal with in a lifetime. You should try to avoid any type of emotional conflict for a time."

Harte didn't look at the therapist. "Look, I don't know who you are or what this place is, or even for sure who this guy Thone is except that he might be responsible for what happened to me. But I do know that your chances of finding where this was done increase dramatically if I'm with you."

The Executioner returned her level gaze full measure.

"And I know that getting out there and being part of the hunting party is going to help me." She took a deep, shuddering breath. "I've been away for years. During that time I've lost a significant portion of my life, my father and maybe a lot of friends. I don't know. But I was a cop once, and I was damn good at my job in spite of whatever your report says about my dismissal." She spread her hands before her. "Maybe I'll see something you won't. Even screwed up as they are, my memories have got to be better than a number of guesses you could make."

"You're up to it?"

"Yes."

"Then that's how we'll do it." Bolan checked his watch and looked at Price. "I want to be ready in twenty minutes."

The mission controller nodded.

Looking at Harte, Bolan asked, "Can you make it?"

There was no hesitation in her voice as she pushed away from the table. "With time to spare."

"SHE'S ALREADY WAITING."

Bolan turned to look at Price as she entered the bedroom on the second story. "How is she?"

"Confident. Anxious. Working really hard to maintain her focus." Price looked out the bulletproof window overlooking the Farm's orchards. "Brookshaus isn't sure if going to Juarez is a good idea."

The warrior finished packing his duffel and zipped it. "Don't see that we have much choice at this point."

Price crossed her arms over her breasts. "I agree. Still, it might be better if I was able to field a larger team down there."

"It would take too long," Bolan replied, sliding the Desert Eagle into shoulder leather, "and it would be too noticeable." He studied the television, which was set into the wall. Stories continued to break about terrorist violence surging up around the world. In L.A., the riots were starting to reach fever pitch.

"There's something else." Price turned to face him. "We were busy going over Phoenix's plans to protect the President in Jerusalem, and the Intel Able turned up regarding Fortress Arms's financing, when Brookshaus completed the inventory of alters locked up inside Harte."

Bolan waited.

"One of the alters was code named Foxglove. Her assignment was to kill the Speaker of the House. During the interview, Brookshaus discovered that Foxglove was waiting for a code word to release her to proceed with the programming."

"Was Brookshaus able to defuse the alter?"

"Maybe. She isn't sure. The alter is too closely laid in over Harte's survival instinct. If that personality is tripped, she's going to kill whoever's around her and pull back into whatever cover she can find and try to carry out the assignment." Price looked at him. "If that happens when she's around you, she'll try to kill you."

"If you find a better way to do this, you let me know."
Bolan shouldered the duffel.

Price came forward and gave him a hug and a brief kiss.
"I will. Until then, you stay hard out there. Wherever he
is, you can bet Hayden Thone is waiting to strike back."

12

Miami, Florida

Alexander De Moray picked the lock on the hotel-room door and let himself inside.

At the other end of the simple room, George Cosgrove turned away from the floor-to-ceiling windows holding a silver hip flask in his hand. His suit coat was draped over the back of the chair at the small desk, and his tie was at half-mast.

"Brognola?" the Treasury man said as he came about. Then his eyes widened in surprise when he saw his visitor.

"Sorry," De Moray said. "He'll be along later." He raised the silenced 10 mm pistol at the end of his arm and squeezed through the clip rapidly. The bullets caught Cosgrove in the chest and shoved him backward. The Kevlar vest stopped them from penetrating, but didn't do much for the blunt trauma.

De Moray's last three rounds slammed through the hollow of Cosgrove's throat and the glass panes. Already dying, the Treasury agent fell back through the shattered windows and plunged to the street seven stories below. Stepping to the broken window, De Moray gazed down at the carnage. The Treasury agent had landed across the hood of a jacked-up Monte Carlo. Startled, the driver swerved into a station wagon.

Coolly De Moray unthreaded the silencer and pocketed the weapon. He left the room, pulling the door shut with a handkerchief on the knob. Whistling an old Hank Williams tune, he walked to the staircase door down the hall and waited.

Less than a minute later, Hal Brognola got off the elevator and approached Cosgrove's door. The big Fed rapped his knuckles on the door and stood waiting.

De Moray smiled. He couldn't have planned the timing better. The desk clerk downstairs would still have the phone records logging the faked message from Brognola to Cosgrove, and he'd placed the call to Brognola himself, saying he was Cosgrove's supervisor and wanted a PR session regarding the Treasury agent's accusations. Brognola had appeared to have everything to gain and nothing to lose.

The Justice man rapped on the door again and checked his watch.

Standing just inside the stairway door, De Moray took out his flip phone and called the security number of the hotel. "Hi. I'm one of the guests in the hotel and I'm not looking to get involved, but I think I heard shots in one of the rooms as I passed by." He could hear the confusion going on in the security room.

"What room?" a dry-voiced male demanded.

De Moray gave Cosgrove's room number. He put the phone away and waited. In less than a minute, a trio of armed security guards in tan shirts and red ties erupted out of the elevator cage with drawn weapons. One of them shouted at Brognola.

Perplexed, the Justice agent placed his palms against the wall and stood still while they searched him.

Satisfied, De Moray started down the stairs. Juarez was only a hop away by private jet. Shutting down the operation there would be only a few hours' work.

DAVID MCCARTER WATCHED the addresses skim by as Calvin James piloted the battered Saab past the Tomb of Simon the Just on Ibn el-Walid. The day had heated up, with no relief in sight. This was also the closest they'd drifted back to the Old City since hitting the Bloody Wind in Haram esh-Sherif.

"Coming up, Cal," the Briton said as he unlimbered two Browning Hi-Powers in the double shoulder holsters.

"I see it." James dropped his foot over the brake and applied it gently.

McCarter eared back the hammers on the semiautomatics but left them in leather. "Keep the motor running. This won't take but a moment."

"Any longer than that," James promised, "and if the Anvil of God doesn't get you, Katz will."

"A cakewalk, laddie buck. There can't be more than five or six of them inside." McCarter studied the crafts shop, noting the shelves of small ceramics in the front window. "A place like this, selling as many souvenirs from Taiwan as it does, has to be a front for something."

The Briton opened the door and got out, pausing long enough to light a cigarette. Then he walked across the curb and the sidewalk, passing into the souvenir shop without hesitation.

There was shade inside the shop, but precious little cool air. A ceiling fan whirled limply overhead. McCarter peered through the racks of coffee mugs, earrings, necklaces, plates and other items, and saw three men leaning behind the tall counter.

"Afternoon, gents," he said affably as he cut the distance.

"May I help you?" one of the men asked. His face and that of one of the other men matched the photos Kurtzman had faxed from the Farm. A fourth man stepped from behind a door in the back.

"I'm looking for the Anvil of God," McCarter said, coming to a stop less than eight feet away.

The words galvanized the men into action, and they turned to face him. "I'm afraid I don't know what you're talking about," the man said, moving closer to the counter.

"Yeah, you do." McCarter made his move as the shopkeeper almost cleared the top of the counter with the mini-Uzi he'd had hidden underneath. He stood his ground and whipped out the Brownings, concentrating on his targets as they went for their guns.

The Hi-Powers bucked in his hands as he triggered them. Gunshots became a gathering swell of rolling thunder as brass tumbled through the air. Concentrating on head shots, he eliminated the possibility of their being saved by body armor worn under their clothing. Two rounds flattened against the Second Chance gear he had on himself, and a bullet whizzed by his left ear.

He fired his last rounds in both guns before the last of the terrorists hit the ground. He ejected both magazines from the pistols then quickly recharged them.

Nothing moved in the rear.

He crossed the room, negotiated the corpses, pausing only long enough to drop the button with the white dove holding an olive branch that had become Phoenix Force's calling card in their attacks on the terrorists since the first raid, and checked the back room. Two AK-47 assault rifles lay across a table. A small cabinet to the right held a cache of weapons and grenades behind a partially open door. A pouch containing a sheaf of papers was to one side. He reached in and took it, sliding it into the waistband of his pants.

Knowing the stone structure of the building would prevent a fire from spreading to the other businesses, McCarter took out an incendiary grenade, slipped the pin and dropped the bomb into the room. He pulled the door shut and headed for the front entrance. Before he made it, the grenade exploded, breaking the door down and throwing a wave of heat over the back of the Briton's neck.

The crowd that had gathered near the front of the shop quickly dispersed as he walked out with his guns in his hands. Footsteps slammed against the pavement, and McCarter turned to face two armed men running at him. One of them he recognized from Kurtzman's debrief.

The Hi-Powers came up in his fists and he shot both men twice. Motor control gone as death raked through them with leaden claws, one of the terrorists crashed through the open door of a tannery while the other knocked over a rolling rack of clothing.

James brought the Saab close to the curb and McCarter got in, the Brownings still in his hands. "Message received?" the ex-SEAL asked as he popped the clutch and jumped in front of a minivan.

"Oh, yeah, mate," McCarter said grimly, looking at the flames twisting through the shop's interior. "We're using the universal language these blokes understand."

Cusseta, Georgia

WHEN CARL LYONS STEPPED in front of his quarry, Captain Wiley Hackshaw turned ghost-white.

The military intelligence officer was dark-complected and had curly black hair on top of his head. The sides and back had been shaved so close the pink skin underneath turned the hair color a soft gray. His mustache was pencil-thin and ended with military exactness at the corners of his mouth. He wore combat boots laced up tight, paratrooper's pants with the cuffs tucked in smartly and a green T-shirt that read Property of the U.S. Army. His dogtags glinted in the afternoon sunshine.

Lyons swept his gaze over the captain's off-base housing. It was located in one of the newer-edition tracks in Cusseta, Georgia, that catered to military personnel at nearby Fort Benning.

The street was quiet, and the house was at the end of a circle drive. Rosebushes crept up the walls on either side of the screened porch. The mailbox had Snoopy sitting on his doghouse in scarf, sunglasses and flying jacket, as if he were hot on the Red Baron's tail.

Pausing before he got into the Mazda RX7 in front of his garage, Hackshaw slipped on a pair of sunglasses and said, "Whatever you're selling, I don't want any. There's a No Soliciting sign posted on the house."

"I'm not here to sell you anything," Lyons said affably. He reached in his jacket pocket and gave the ID Price had arranged a workout. "Lambert. I'm with the Justice Department. I've got a few questions I'd like to ask you concerning Hayden Thone and the information you've been giving him."

A sick smile twisted Hackshaw's lower face. "I'm afraid I don't know what you're talking about."

Lyons stopped near the rear bumper of the sports car. "That's not the way Allard Savitch tells it."

The uncertain smile faded. "You got a warrant?"

"No. I figured you might want to cooperate on your own."

"You figured wrong." Hackshaw clambered into the Mazda and tried to put the key into the ignition.

Lyons slipped his Swiss army knife from his pocket, flicked out a blade with a thumbnail and slashed the rear tire. It went flat with a sibilant whoosh.

"You son of a bitch!" Hackshaw roared, coming out of the car with a .45 clenched in his fist.

Lyons knew the man wouldn't hesitate about firing. Hackshaw had no family, no ties to keep him to the city or his career if he knew he was busted. A little running room and he'd be gone.

Stepping forward, the big Able Team warrior caught the man's gun hand as he erupted from the car. Lyons twisted, bringing the captain's fingers near the breaking point. The gun came free in his hand and he immediately reversed it, settling the muzzle against Hackshaw's forehead. The hammer triple-clicked as he brought it back with a thumb.

"Your choice," he said in a thin, cold voice.

"Okay. Just don't shoot. Sometime's that thing's got a hair trigger."

"Give me a wrist." Lyons snapped his handcuffs on the arm thrust out at him, turned Hackshaw around against the sports car, kicked his feet apart and cuffed the other arm behind his back.

"Ironman!" Blancanales roared over the headset.

Immediately Lyons went to ground, dragging his prisoner with him. Autofire raked the Mazda, punching out fist-size holes in the windshield and glass and ripping tears in the bodywork. Rubber shrilled on the street.

Gazing under the parked car, Lyons saw the full-size Mercury alter its course and race toward the Mazda. A gunner hung outside the passenger window with an Ingram chattering in his arms. Beyond them, already responding but precious heartbeats behind, Schwarz dropped into gear the Isuzu Trooper they'd pulled for the assignment, and raced off in pursuit.

Lyons got to his feet, glancing over the hood of the Mazda as the Mercury sped toward them, growing larger. He yanked Hackshaw up. "Move!" he growled. He dragged the man after him, racing toward the protection of the garage. A cinder-block wall jutted only a few feet away. They'd almost made it when the Mercury smashed into the smaller car.

The sports car slowed the sedan just enough to allow Lyons time to yank his captive around the corner of the wall. Shoving Hackshaw behind him, Lyons watched the cinder-block wall as the sound of rending metal closed on them.

The wall didn't hold, either. Cinder blocks came flying free and raked the front of the house like shrapnel, busting out the windows and beating down the rosebushes. The rolling onslaught of metal plowed over the Snoopy mailbox and dug up the underground sprinkler system. Water sprayed into the air and came down in fat drops.

Raising the .45, Lyons fired twice at the gunner taking cover on the passenger side of the Mercury. The Mazda butted up against the screened porch. Both rounds hit the guy on the passenger side, and blood splashed over the inside of the windshield.

"Get down and stay down!" he commanded Hackshaw, kicking the man's feet out from under him. He switched hands, then drew his own .45 as he advanced on the tangle of cars and house.

The rear window on the passenger side shattered and came apart as a man back there fired through.

Lyons returned fire without hesitation. He was aware of the Trooper rolling to a stop a few feet away and Blancanales dropping out of the door with a Remington 870 pump shotgun in his hands.

The driver leaped free of the Mercury and brought his Uzi around in a sweep that chewed an arc of bullets across the Trooper's windshield. Then Blancanales's shotgun blammed once and stretched a dead man across the sedan's hood. Before he could bring the 12-gauge back to cover the rear door, the other gunner fired.

Caught somewhere high and outside, Blancanales spun and lost his footing.

Schwarz came around the Trooper at a dead run, his Beretta 92-F held in both hands as he dropped the pistol into target acquisition. He fired four times. None of them missed. A dead man tumbled free of the Mercury.

His guns level before him, Lyons approached the sedan. A quick glance assured him that the Mercury had become a coffin.

"Pol," Lyons called out.

Having trouble getting to a sitting position, Blancanales looked down at his right arm. Blood spilled into the crook of his elbow from a wound high on his biceps. "I'm okay," he said. "Through and through, and it doesn't look like the bone or an artery was hit."

Schwarz grabbed the first-aid kit from the Trooper and went to attend his partner. Up and down the small street, mothers were still hurrying their children into the houses.

Anger touched Lyons when he saw the action. He recrossed the yard to Hackshaw. "This probably used to be a good place to live before you got here, slimeball." He yanked the man to his feet and pushed him back against the cracked garage wall. "In case you're a little slow as well as greedy, I'd say Hayden Thone has reached the conclusion that you're a risky investment and has decided to ace you. You see it any other way, maybe you'd like to take your chances here for a while before I arrest you."

"No."

"You try withholding on me," Lyons promised, "about any of the information I want concerning those Grand Cayman accounts, and you and I are coming back here together to search through your house. We'll stay here until Thone sends another group. Only this time I might not be so quick to save your ass."

"I'll talk."

Lyons gave the man a hard stare, then grabbed him by the arm to lead him away, and said, "Start now. We're burning daylight here."

Stony Man Farm

"—ATTACKS AGAINST Palestinian terrorist splinter groups continue here in Jerusalem," the news anchor from BBC commented in neutral tones. He was thin and dapper in his dark suit, neatly clipped hair blowing in the breeze. Behind him, sunset had colored the western sky beyond Jerusalem, glinting off the gold-colored domes, minarets and tall buildings. The camera crew had set up on Mount Scopus, Barbara Price guessed as she stood and gazed at the wall screen at the end of the large computer room.

Aaron Kurtzman sat at the horseshoe-shaped desk on a dais overlooking the section of Stony Man Farm that was under his direct control. He worked the computer console in front of him, referring to the three monitors arranged on the desktop.

"Their symbol is this," the anchor went on. He held up a pale blue disk with a white dove holding an olive branch in its beak. The camera zoomed in for a close-up. "No one knows who these people represent, and their number has been guessed at somewhere between fifteen and fifty, but their objective is clear—they're issuing a warning to terrorist groups who would interfere in the peace talks between Israel and the legal representatives of the Palestinian people. And that warning brooks no misinterpretation. UN forces in the area are all accounted for, and—despite protests from several groups sympathetic to the terrorists—have not been involved in the outbreak of violence. But they are searching for this phantom force delivering terror to the terrorists."

"Sounds like Katz and Phoenix are out there kicking butt and taking names," Akira Tokaido said from the floor. His computer console was closest to the center wall screen. Although of Japanese ancestry, the youngest member of Kurtzman's handpicked computer team had spent all his life in the United States. No one, including Kurtzman, knew how many computer systems Tokaido had crashed illegally before being recruited to the Stony Man Farm project. But now he did them with sanction, and it was almost magic to watch him work intuitively through the different systems.

To the right, Huntington Wethers, the black ex-professor of cybernetics at Berkeley University, sat back in his chair and removed the pipe he'd been chewing. Gray at his temples lent him a distinguished look. "Aaron."

Kurtzman looked up. "Yeah."

"I've traced back the bank accounts that Hackshaw gave Able Team, but I can't get very far. Those accounts were set up in the Grand Caymans during the savings-and-loan fiascos of the 1980s. It's a morass trying to get through them. Government intervention only made the problem worse."

"It usually does," Carmen Delahunt commented from the final workstation to the left of the room. She was a fiery redhead with workhorse stamina, old-line FBI recruited from Quantico, Virginia.

"Stay with it, Hunt," Kurtzman said. "If Akira gets anything more from those damaged files, he'll give it to you. Find me a hook to hang this whole mess on."

Wethers nodded, massaged the back of his neck and went back to work.

At the other end of the room, the wall screen shifted, letting the BBC story in Jerusalem shrink down to a window as it opened up other windows across the surface. Price watched them with interest. A feeling of paranoia had already settled into the media reports, but the electronic sources were feeding the frenzy the most, filling television screens across nations with scenes of violence and death.

Even with the proof they had, linking Hayden Thone, Fortress Arms and the alters to the pattern of violence was impossible. UN forces were stretched tight across the globe. Although seemingly intangible and invisible, the mission controller knew a malevolent hand was constricting its hold on the world.

"What are you thinking about?" Kurtzman asked, never missing a beat in his work.

"The Foxglove personality in Harte."

"What about it?"

"If all the alters are programmed with that kind of hidden agenda, there'll be hell to pay if Thone puts it into play. If an assassin is willing to give his or her life to get to a target, you can't protect that target. And what bothers me is why he hasn't already put it into play."

Acting the part of the devil's advocate, Kurtzman said, "It's possible it's not as easily activated as we might fear, or it's possible that he's wanting to pick a time that will be more strategically effective." He glanced up at her as the computer screens in front of him filled with new information. "And it's possible that the son of a bitch is taking his time to enjoy it."

"Megalomania."

"Fits everything I've seen in the guy. If he'd stayed small-time in Europe supplying illegal arms, he'd have made a goodly fortune. Instead, he had to branch out, come to America and set up shop here, hobnobbing with the Hollywood crowd."

"It was more than that," Price said. "He changed businesses. At first he was satisfied with running guns, then he became obsessed with applied terrorism. That's why he invested in the alters so heavily."

"In his line of work, terrorism makes good business. But I agree with you—he likes it for the control, too."

"Aaron."

Price and Kurtzman looked up at Wethers.

"I got something here."

Kurtzman tapped his keyboard and brought data online. "Explain it to me."

"It's kind of convoluted, but bear with me. In 1980 when Thone made the move from Germany to America, he transferred monies through other accounts in the Grand Caymans. I got into some old files down there. The accounts were operated under dozens of different names, and for a while the money jumped back and forth from one to the other like an active pinball trapped between bumpers. The DEA nearly tagged him twice."

"Drug money?" Price asked.

"Thone received it. Probably for guns. But the DEA didn't have enough to investigate quickly. By the time they did, Thone must have been tipped off, because the accounts disappeared like morning mist."

"Don't tell me you're just teasing me," Kurtzman said.

Wethers grinned. "I don't tease unless I can please. Check this out." He worked the keyboard.

Price watched closely but quickly felt like she was watching an expert street huckster working a game of three-card monte. Statement after statement concerning bank account transactions filled the screen.

"I've got it reduced to seconds," Wethers said, "but the chain is complete. Real time, this series covers five years, seven months and a week or two."

"Bottom line," Kurtzman said.

"Fortress Arms bought a piece of property in Ciudad Juarez in 1984 and spent a considerable amount improving it. I cross-referenced the property, accessed four banks I have ingress to and came up with this."

Kurtzman's screen cleared, leaving the name of a business scrawled across it: Gildalho Trading Company.

"In the 1930s," Wethers said, continuing, "the trading company was a legitimate business. It went under in the early 1960s and has pretty much sat vacant since that time."

"And now?" Price prompted.

Wethers smiled. "And now Gildalho Trading Company pays *mucho dinero* in utilities but doesn't seem to do any business domestically or internationally."

"Good work, Hunt." Price took up the cellular phone from the hip holster at her side and started to punch in the car-phone number she had for the Executioner.

"Barb," Carmen Delahunt called out. "It's Hal on line four. He says it's urgent."

Price lifted one of the phones on Kurtzman's desk and pressed the flashing light. "Price."

"Look," Brognola said in a tense tone, "I don't have much time. A couple hours of ago I was arrested for the murder of George Cosgrove, the Treasury agent I've been having the run-ins with down here. They just processed me and made it official. This is my one phone call."

The mission controller didn't doubt for a moment that Hayden Thone had reached out from his hiding place to put Brognola in jeopardy. The stakes had been raised, and she knew she couldn't falter.

Austria

"I THINK you're dodging shadows."

Hayden Thone stood at the bulletproof windows of his bedroom in the ancestral castle his grandfather had stubbornly clung to even when the family business had been foundering, and looked down the steep, snow-covered slopes to the northwest. He didn't let De Moray's words anger him and kept his hand loose on the phone. "When the rest of the day has passed, you can tell me that. Until then, you people stay ready down there.''

De Moray chuckled. "Actually I hope that big son of a bitch does show up here. It would be interesting to see who's really better, me or him.''

"Lex, you're not into challenges. You live for the kill. Don't get overconfident and disappoint me. We've carved ourselves an empire over these past years. Let's try to live long enough to enjoy the fruits of our labors.'' Thone turned away from the window. A fire was blazing in the fireplace, and Mancuso tended the logs with focused attention and a poker he wielded like an épée.

The furniture was a collection of dark woods from the days of the German confederation. Although he'd never found out if his grandfather was telling the truth, the roll-top desk under the shield bearing the Thone family crest was supposed to have been used by Otto von Bismarck. Thick woolen rugs covered the stone floor. In the center of the room, a four-poster sat on a raised wooden dais, draped with lace curtains. Recessed track lighting provided discreet illumination.

Thone liked the castle only because his grandfather had coveted it so. He preferred American decadence and room service. But for now, the castle was a secure place in the world, away from the uncertainties posed by the covert strike force hunting him. The attack plans in Jerusalem had pretty well been reduced to a shambles.

He dropped into a thick, ornate sofa that was part of the group in front of the fireplace. After replacing the poker, Mancuso crossed to the full-service bar against the wall and poured himself a fresh glass of wine. The Sicilian had never cared for the winter climate prevalent in the mountains.

"What about Brognola?" Thone asked.

"He's been arrested by the Dade County Sheriff's Office," De Moray answered.

"Do his people know yet?"

"They should. Reporters are starting to break the story in the media."

"Are we going to be able to get to him?"

"Within the next few hours. Easy."

"I want to know as soon as it's done."

"No problem."

"And stay sharp down there, Lex. We don't know what resources these people have open to them at this time."

De Moray broke the connection without comment.

Standing in front of the fire, swirling his glass of wine in open speculation, Mancuso said, "You know, Hayden, it might be in our best interests to simply withdraw from the game and live off our ill-gotten gains."

"Without discovering if all the money we invested in the alter programming was worth it?"

"Yes."

"You surprise me, old friend. In all the long years of our association, you've constantly harped at me to make sure I got full value for every dollar, mark, yen and pound that I ever spent." Thone pushed himself up from the sofa and poured himself a shot of schnapps. It burned all the way down, and he poured another.

"Before, we've always been up against people that money meant something to," Mancuso said. He pointed at the large-screen television across the room that played footage from the lightning attacks against Palestinian terrorists in Jerusalem. "It doesn't mean anything to the men behind this. There's no one we can buy off or leverage political pressure against."

"They still bleed," Thone said stubbornly. "And they'll die when the time comes for that as well. Idealism doesn't work in this world anymore. We've been teetering on the

edge of total anarchy for so long that the entire planet is in
denial. The United States has portrayed itself as a global
supercop. Events in Panama, the Gulf War and Eastern
Europe have furthered that belief. But it's a lie."

Mancuso said nothing.

Thone returned to the room's other window and peered
down. The castle wasn't large as castles went, but it was
relatively secluded in the Central Alps. The Grossglock-
ner was less than five miles away, while Innsbruck was
nearly a hundred to the west. Outside, snow swirled and
started falling again, adding to the twenty-nine-inch
foundation that had already been built up. Armed guards
patrolled the open courtyard two floors below, as well as
the twelve-foot walls enclosing the castle grounds.

"I told you about my experiences during the 1972
Olympics in Munich," Thone said. His breath fogged the
bulletproof glass in front of him. "I saw firsthand the effects terrorism has on people. The Israelis were unforgiving, and tracked down the members of Black September
until they had them all. The world might remember Mark
Spitz and the seven gold medals he won in swimming, but
it will never forget the blood that was spilled." He sipped
the schnapps. "We're animals, living together in an in-
creasingly smaller environment. Territorial aggression is a
natural thing and can't be ignored. There's a world of
frightened people out there, wondering what the economy
is going to do to them. The economy is something they
can't fight. Hell, most of them don't even understand it.
But they're willing to do battle with their neighbors, and
you can bet they'll be more willing as jobs become in-
creasingly scarce. I'm just going to make sure they're better equipped when the time comes."

"You could use the Foxglove alters at any time," Mancuso pointed out. "There's no reason to use them now."

"On the contrary." Thone felt the anger burning white-hot in him as he turned to face his friend. "I've been chased and hounded from my home in America for simply doing business that governments have been doing for decades. The Americans don't have unsullied hands. They've supplied arms the world over to whomever they wanted to support while they've tried to protect the world from communism and Middle Eastern despots. I'm probably the most nonpartisan arms dealer in operation today. The U.S. and Europe deserve the carnage that's going to erupt after the Foxglove objectives are met."

Outside, the moon broke through the cloud cover for just a moment and burned down bright and hard.

"Television and computers may have drawn the world closer, and CNN might bring viewers global events in seconds, but none of them can smooth over the primitive that beats inside every human heart." Thone glanced at Mancuso. "I believe there's only a thin veneer of civilization left spread over the world. And come morning, when the President is on hand to help with the peace talks in Israel, I intend to find out. When the dust clears, we'll find out if the President is still standing and can continue meddling in world affairs."

13

Mexico

At one time, the Gildalho Trading Company had occupied an affluent part of Juarez. Kurtzman's findings had revealed that. But those days were long gone. Now it sat in the middle of one of the many red-light districts that ran rampant through the border town.

Mack Bolan sat behind the wheel of the dark blue Mitsubishi 3000GT VR-4, concealed in the shadows by a closed garage half a block down from Lady Rangers Strip Club.

He used the night glasses from his vest and surveyed the back of the trading company across the street. The windows had been painted black, and there was no sign of light around the doors. It was built like an old-time aircraft hangar in dome shape. Hammered metal covered it, looking weathered and worn in places, and grayed-out to the point that it almost faded into the gathering dusk.

The sun had set minutes ago, leaving only scarlet, gold and lavender stains against the cobalt-blue sky. True dark would descend in heartbeats, held at bay by the neon forest.

"It's underground." Giselle Harte leaned up from the narrow seat in the back of the sports car.

Bolan locked eyes with her in the rearview mirror. "Basement?"

She shook her head. "It's more than a basement. There's a couple floors hidden under there." Her hair was pulled back and piled on top of her head under a Houston Astros baseball cap. Black body armor covered the blacksuit and linked up with the combat webbing she wore.

"Excavation was possible," Jack Grimaldi said from the passenger seat. He was outfitted in combat black and body armor, as well. The pilot pointed down the street. "Thone also owns Trujillo Construction."

Bolan looked. The construction site held a half dozen yellow earth movers, and hills of sand and gravel inside a ten-foot mesh fence, which was topped by security lights and barbed wire.

"Figure a tunnel maybe a block and a half long," Grimaldi went on, "and the excavation would never have shown up. They could have sold the dirt they removed or simply dumped it somewhere else. No one would have asked questions seeing dump trucks leaving with loads."

Traffic was light along the back street.

"However it was done," the warrior said, "we're going in." He popped the dome light out of its socket and hit the door release. The car interior stayed dark as he got out.

Clad in a blacksuit, he looked like a shadow. Taking a tin of combat cosmetics from the car pocket, he applied it in tiger stripes with ease, working his face by touch. When he was through, he tossed the tin to Grimaldi, who darkened his own features, then those of Harte.

The ex-policewoman was holding up well on the outside, but Bolan could feel the inner tension.

Moving to the back of the Mitsubishi 3000GT, he opened the trunk and reached inside for the gear stored there. Price had arranged for the car in El Paso, and for the hardware on the other side of the border. The conversation had been brief and to the point because the mission controller had been involved in coordinating Able Team's and Phoenix Force's efforts in Miami and Jerusalem. He stayed away from thoughts about Brognola being unprotected in the Dade County lockup.

The body armor he wore allowed him to affix pouches for grenades, handcuffs, extra magazines, shotgun shells, a gas mask and the collapsible grappling hook with nylon rope. He carried the Beretta 93-R at his back in a kidney pouch so it wouldn't interfere with the gear he had across his chest. The Desert Eagle rode his thigh in a counterterrorist drop holster. For a lead weapon he carried the Franchi PA-3 215 pump-action 12-gauge shotgun with folding stock.

Harte took the Remington Model 870 from the trunk. It was chopped down and equipped with a pistol grip, modified by Cowboy John Kissinger—the Farm's weapons expert—with a skeletal folding stock in the event of prolonged use. Grimaldi chose the silenced Ingram MAC-10.

"Jack," Bolan said as he fitted the ear-throat headset under the fold-away hood and pulled it into place, "you've got the front. Nobody in or out once we open the door on this. The object is to keep it quiet as long as we can. After we open the ball, detonate the charges you'll be putting around the building and let's generate as much confusion on this as we can."

"Right." The pilot gathered his weapon close to his chest and jogged across the street.

Bolan watched the rear of the Gildalho Trading Company. No movement caught his eye. Seconds later, he took the lead and sprinted to the back of the building. Scanning the structure, he found the power lines leading to a sophisticated security system designed to trigger an alarm when the building's integrity was breached.

He let the Franchi shotgun hang from its sling while he used his multipurpose tool to skin the wires and bypass the system with alligator clips.

"Not really much in the way of security," Harte commented. Perspiration made her face glow in the places not covered by the cosmetic.

"They've been here a long time," Bolan replied as he forced the door lock. It clicked in his hands and he pushed it open slightly. Warm air rushed out at him. "Security has gotten lax." Whisper-soft, the numbers on the mission began trickling through his mind.

"Three people against God knows how many seems like long odds."

"No other way to do it. Insertion of any more troops down here would definitely be noticed." The warrior eased inside the building, noting the bulky shapes of ancient packing equipment in the center of the warehouse. Against the wall to the left, stacks of wooden crates and bales of moldy straw leaned against one another. The musty smell of machine oil, gasoline and straw pervaded the huge room. At the far end, dimly visible in the dark and broken only by low-wattage bulbs staggered along a suspended power line, was a small office with a large window broken into shards that gray duct tape held in place.

Harte followed close behind the Executioner as they entered the building and avoided the pools of weak yellow light.

A lighter flared to the right, less than twenty feet in front of them, revealing a stocky man with swarthy features and a Mini-14 Ranch Rifle hanging at his side. He saw Bolan and Harte a moment after the warrior saw him.

Instantly the Executioner moved into action. Knowing that there were probably innocents in the concealed floors below who would be killed outright, he swept the Beretta out of the kidney pouch and fired three shots. The silencer made coughing noises as the pistol jumped in his fist. All three parabellum rounds crunched into the man's forehead, knocking him to the floor.

Moving forward to ascertain the kill, Bolan tapped the transmit button on the headset. "G-Force."

"Go," Grimaldi returned.

"We've had contact."

"Affirmative. You yell, I'll come running."

Glancing back over his shoulder as he dragged the dead man to the side out of the light, Bolan saw the pallor that had settled over Harte's features. "There're no constraints about deadly force here tonight. If you don't understand that, your place is outside."

She shook her head. "I'm okay. I came here to see this through."

He clapped her on the shoulder. "Then let's get it done. Where's the door?"

Her brow furrowed and she scanned the darkness. "That office. I think. It's hard to remember. So many things are fuzzy."

"We'll start there." Bolan took the lead and they moved quietly into the office.

The desk, chair and shelves were relatively clear of dust. One of the shelves held an AM-FM receiver with headphones and a small twelve-inch black-and-white television. Using his penlight conservatively, Bolan located the hidden door artificed into the shelves. Evidently over the years the hinges had loosened and allowed the door to drag over the floor, gouging a ninety-degree arc on the concrete. The trip switch was a lever concealed as part of the facing on the shelves. It moved smoothly.

With only a small creak, the hidden door swung forward.

Bolan kept the Franchi on the opening. Only the skeletal frame of a circular stairway filled the door. A ghostly fluorescent light glowed from somewhere below.

"Sarge," Grimaldi called out.

"Go," Bolan said as he started down the stairs.

"The charges are placed. I've got your flank covered."

"Roger. Can you find the power-line hookups?"

"I tied into them for juice."

"Right after you blow the front doors, I want the power shut down."

"You got it."

Bolan came to a stop at the foot of the stairs where a short wall ended abruptly a few feet farther on. The light was more intense around the corner. The air was crisp and clean, almost too cool.

Peering around the corner, Bolan saw that the narrow hallway opened up into a large room. Beyond it were three doors. He stepped forward, knowing he was operating on borrowed time.

The first door on his right was labeled Security, Unauthorized Persons Stay Out. He tried the knob and found it unlocked. The warrior pushed the door open and surprised the two men at the four stacked security monitors that flicked constantly through a series of views. One of them was the stairway Harte and Bolan had just descended.

One of the men went for the pistol holstered at his side.

Without hesitation, the Executioner squeezed the Beretta's trigger twice, putting rounds through the man's temple.

The corpse spun in the swivel chair and dropped onto the floor.

Bolan shifted the pistol's muzzle to the second man. "He's made his last mistake," he said in a graveyard voice. "How about you?"

Reluctantly the man raised his hands.

"Down on the floor," the warrior commanded. When the man complied, Harte cuffed him with practiced ease. Perspiration dotted the woman's forehead, and her hands shook as she straightened.

She caught him looking. "I'm okay. Just memories crowding in, giving me a headache."

"Keep an eye on the door."

She took up position.

Directing his attention to the surviving guard, Bolan took a seat behind the security console and pulled the computer keyboard toward him. The security configuration was fairly standard and gave him no problems when he accessed it through the computer. On-line now, he lifted the phone to his left, dialed a number for Stony Man Farm and got put through to Kurtzman.

"Ready," the computer expert assured him.

Bolan dropped the phone receiver onto the modem. The mainframe's hard disk started cycling through at once. The security monitors froze for a moment, wavered, then started cycling through again, letting him know Kurtzman had looped into that system as well and would be providing additional information as needed. He adjusted the headset's frequency until he located the one Kurtzman had access to. "I'm here," he said.

"Check," Kurtzman rumbled.

Going back to the initial frequency, Bolan alerted Grimaldi to the channel change, then rejoined the Stony Man Farm computer expert. "How much time are you going to need?"

"I don't know," Kurtzman replied. "There's a mother lode of information in this system, but I'm not sure what the menus mean. I'm going to yank as much of it as I can and try to sort it out later."

"Unless there's an alternate power source," the warrior said, "it'll go down when we blow the fuse boxes."

"Do what you have to. I'll do the same here." Kurtzman paused. "I found eight people on the second floor that are in some kind of ward."

"Show me," Harte said, leaning in toward the monitors.

The top left monitor fuzzed out for a moment, then refocused on a room that glowed with twilight and was filled with hospital beds. Bolan couldn't make out much detail about the persons in the beds, but he could see the array of computer hardware and medical equipment hooked up to the individuals. Most of them looked like they were wrapped in rubber and wiring.

"That's the room," Harte said.

Bolan glanced at her. The tone in her voice made it clear what room it was.

Kurtzman's voice held reverence. "That's next-generation virtual-reality hardware. I'm looking at the schematics on it now. With that stuff, coupled with the drugs and psychological attacks, they could make a person believe anything or remember events that never happened to them."

"Can you get me a map?" Bolan asked.

"Sure." The monitor on the lower left rippled, then unfurled diagrams of the two subterranean floors. "I'm also going through the security cameras in order to get you a head count."

Bolan memorized the maps, and started to turn from the monitors when he heard the footstep in the outside hallway. Spinning, he caught sight of the man using the door frame as cover while he brought up a nickel-plated Dan Wesson .41 Magnum.

Not trusting his 9 mm pistol to penetrate the modular walls, the Executioner flexed his arm and yanked on the sling. The Franchi PA-3 215 came easily to hand. He squeezed the trigger and the deep-throated boom crashed over the electronic hum of the computer systems.

The 12-gauge shot pattern ripped a plate-size hole in the wall as it blew the gunner against the opposite wall.

Bolan racked the slide, sending the empty shell whirling, and moved toward the door. He tapped the headset's transmit button. "G-Force."

"Go."

"They know we're here."

"Just tell me when."

"I will." Taking up a position by the door, Bolan peered through the smoking hole in the wall. Someone tripped an alarm. A screaming siren rent the air like an angry banshee.

Two gunners ran up the hallway toward the security room.

Bolan leaned around the door and fired three rounds, holding down the trigger as he pumped the slide. The double-aught buckshot caught the men and twisted them like leaves in a spring wind. The warrior thumbed fresh shells into the Franchi as he sprinted out of the security room toward the three doors open to him. Harte was close behind.

He picked the door on the right, knowing from the map that the stairway leading to the bottom floor was just beyond. The door was locked. Stepping back, he aimed the shotgun at the lock at point-blank range and loosed a blast.

Metal sparked and became a smoking, warped ruin.

He kicked at the door and felt it jar open. Harte's shotgun boomed behind him, and he caught sight of a gunner tumbling to the floor from the periphery of his vision. The landing beyond the door was small and ringed by a metal frame.

A man was racing up the steps, his boots ringing on the metal. He saw Bolan, raised his assault rifle to his shoulder and opened fire.

A fistful of 5.56 mm tumblers sprayed past the Executioner as he ducked. He extended the Franchi the length of his arm and held it one-handed. When he squeezed the trigger, the foot-long muzzle-flash licked at the man's face. The corpse was thrown over the railing.

Getting to his feet, the Executioner racked the slide and pumped a shell into the chamber. He yanked a CS gas grenade from the armor, pulled the pin and dropped the canister onto the landing. "Let's go," he growled to Harte.

For a moment, she seemed frozen. Then she stumbled into a start.

Bolan followed her. Halfway down the staircase, the grenade exploded, releasing a sickly yellow cloud that quickly enveloped the landing. A man burst through the broken door and raised his pistol. Before he could fire, the tear gas bit into his lungs and drove him back into the other room.

Harte took the lead through the door at the bottom of the staircase. Trailing close behind, Bolan managed the rearguard and wing coverage.

"Striker!" Kurtzman roared over the headset.

"Go."

"They've got an ambush waiting on you at the end of the corridor."

Spotting the security camera mounted on the wall at the end of the hallway, Bolan snagged an HE grenade from his vest. Harte showed no sign of hearing the warning. Digging for the extra speed, he threw himself at her. He wrapped an arm around her as shadows moved at the end of the corridor, and bore her down like a lineman sacking a quarterback. They slid along the polished floor and collided painfully with the wall.

He flipped the grenade in an underhand toss across the floor and pulled the woman back into the protection of a recessed door. Bullets stitched the hallway, strafing the floor, searching for them.

Then the grenade went off, a mammoth thunderclap that deafened the warrior. He was on his feet at once, the Franchi in both hands as he raced to secure the corridor. Ears ringing with the noise from the explosion, he could see the yelling man suddenly appear in front of him but couldn't hear him. The Executioner fired on the run.

The double-aught charge caught the gunner in the chest and punched him back into the man behind him.

Racking the slide, Bolan fired again, cutting down the man struggling to shove the corpse off. Three hardmen were waiting around the corner, bearing wounds from the grenade blast.

The man on his right came up with a machine pistol blazing in his fist.

Ducking to one side, the Executioner fired the two remaining rounds in the Franchi, blowing the man away. Before he could recover, the gunner on the left came at him, the 9 mm pistol in his hand pointed at Bolan's head. Recoiling, the warrior swept out with the empty shotgun and broke his attacker's wrist. Bringing the Franchi back across, he landed another blow on the man's jaw and knocked him cold.

The surviving gunner tried to dodge his falling comrade and bring up the .45 pistol in his hands.

Squaring off with the man, Bolan dropped the Franchi and let it hang from his shoulder by its sling. His hand drifted down and drew the Desert Eagle smoothly from his hip. Yellow-and-white muzzle-flash leaped from the gunner's weapon.

The .45-caliber bullet smashed into the Strike Face ceramic plate covering Bolan's sternum with enough force to stagger him. Triggering two rounds, he watched the 240-grain boattails take the man in the face and throat and spin him away.

When he glanced around, he found Harte standing behind him with her shotgun at the ready. Tapping the headset's transmit button, he said, "Stony Base, I don't know if you can read me, but we're taking this operation down. G-Force, I can't respond because I can't pick up your transmission, but set those charges off now." He moved out along the new hallway. A heartbeat later the underground complex shivered and shook as the plastic explosive went off.

The lights flickered and went out, replaced suddenly by the emergency spots.

He didn't bother with the shotgun as he jogged along, filling his hands with his pistols. Two men exited from different doors ahead of him. He fired from the point, crashing out death that hammered them to the floor.

Moving to the entrance on the right, he shoved the door open and scanned the room. Two emergency floodlights shone down from opposite walls on either side, playing over the hospital beds that held men and women strapped down. Flat-lensed goggles covered their eyes, and electrode patches were wrapped around their fingers and toes while others were flush with skin on their chests, arms and legs. Some of the unwilling patients jumped and jerked as they twisted against their bonds.

"Welcome to my parlor, said the spider to the fly." At the other end of the room, past the double row of hospital beds, a man stepped out of the shadows into the uncertain glow of the floodlights.

Bolan recognized Alexander De Moray from his pictures and the close brush they'd had in Monte Carlo. He kept his pistols at the ready, knowing the man wouldn't blatantly step into the open without an ace hidden somewhere. Harte stepped into his shadow but stayed beyond the periphery of the warrior's vision.

"Also, welcome to the Wild Hunt," De Moray added. He stood his ground, a mocking smile playing on his lips. Dressed in a black duster and dark clothing, he looked as if he grew up from the pool of darkness at his feet—except for the cold silver glare of the S&W 1006 10 mm pistol clenched in his fist at his side. He waved his free hand toward the people in the hospital beds. "These are my disciples. Ready, willing, and soon to be able to go out in the world and act in my name."

Bolan lowered the Beretta and tucked it into his waistband. The Desert Eagle still held four rounds in its magazine, and he wanted a free hand. His hearing was coming back, though it still sounded as if De Moray were talking from the bottom of a very deep well. "They won't after tonight."

"That depends. Are you prepared to sacrifice them to stop me?"

Bolan didn't reply.

"I take it that's a no. You can't fight a war against someone with your hands tied behind your back. I've tried." De Moray shrugged. "I don't care if these people live or die. You do. That puts me in a position to bargain."

"Get me to the bottom line." Bolan's voice was graveyard cold, and the Desert Eagle never wavered in his fist.

"I walk out of here, live to fight another day."

"I don't think so."

De Moray laughed. "Haven't you learned by now? You can't catch the Huntsman."

"But I have."

The Cajun shrugged, his face mocking. "You make your play for me, and I'll kill these people." He held up his free hand like a magician plucking coins from the air. A squared-off box with a glowing readout showed against his palm. "Remote-control detonator. Those beds are wired. I push a button, you'll be picking these people up with a stick and a spoon."

Bolan eased down the .44's hammer.

"Good choice, my friend." De Moray walked forward slowly, still holding the device in clear view.

"You could still trigger the explosives once you hit the street," the Executioner said.

"Maybe the signal won't transmit this far. Or maybe you can trust me."

"No." Bolan let the distance drop to twenty feet. De Moray was between the hospital beds, halfway down. He rolled the hammer back with his thumb again.

The Cajun smiled. "You won't do that. My friend Cassandra won't let you."

Bolan felt Harte shift behind him, then the heated muzzle of her shotgun settled at the base of his skull.

"Don't you just love the alternative way of living some people have?" De Moray asked. "Just when you think you know who your friends are, they change, and you suddenly discover you don't know them at all."

"I'll live long enough to pull this trigger," the Executioner promised.

De Moray shook his head in mock perplexity. "You don't understand the Wild Hunt at all, do you?" He took another step forward, more slowly.

"You're wrong about her," Bolan said. "She's changed. She's not yours anymore. She's seen through the lies you gave her."

"She'll pull the trigger when I tell her to. The Wild Hunt is real, and it's death incarnate. Just like me. These people are all lost souls waiting to be just like me. Inside every man and woman lives a killer screaming to get out. We're all predators."

"You're wrong," the Executioner said. "Inside every man and woman is a warrior that will step out to do battle when the time comes. Some are predators, but they're the exception rather than the rule."

"And where do you fit in?"

"I'm a hunter. Where most people have the ability and fortitude to fight for themselves in their personal battles, there are some who can't. I hunt down the predators they can't stand against."

"Pious prick, aren't you?" De Moray took another step. "How are you going to feel when you have to shoot her to keep her from killing you?"

"She won't try," Bolan said. "Giselle, it's time to come back. There's only one Huntsman in this room, and he's standing in front of you. Look past the lies."

De Moray shook his head. "Shoot him! Shoot him now!"

Abruptly the shotgun barrel swept away from Bolan's neck. He didn't hesitate, changing his aim slightly and squeezing the Desert Eagle's trigger.

The 240-grain bullet hit De Moray in the wrist of the hand that held the device, nearly amputating the hand. Screaming in pain and rage, knocked halfway around by the muzzle velocity of the .44 round, he struggled to bring up the S&W 1006.

Bolan fired the remaining three rounds in the big pistol, hearing an echoing thunderclap from Harte's shotgun. Propelled backward by the force of the blast, De Moray crashed against the foot of a bed and lay still, his face almost blown away.

The sirens were still wailing out in the hallway as Bolan fed a fresh magazine into the pistol and turned to face the woman. Pain and anguish showed in her eyes. "It's over," he said softly. "Nothing to be afraid of anymore."

"I almost shot you," she said. "I couldn't help myself. It was like I was in the back of my mind with a front-row seat to the whole thing. I came so close."

Bolan put a comforting arm around her shoulders. "But you didn't."

She looked down at De Moray, then slowly approached as if afraid the dead man would suddenly jump up to live again. "How did you know the remote control wouldn't detonate?"

"I got a better look at it than he thought," Bolan said. He nudged the device with his toe and flipped it over so the keys showed. "It was a calculator."

"Sarge," Grimaldi called over the headset frequency.

"Go."

"The local constabulary is taking an active interest in our party here. You really want to stay around to talk?"

"We're on our way." Bolan looked at the woman.

"A moment," she said, fishing in her pockets. She took the key case out with the Vietnamese beer cap and dropped it onto De Moray's chest. "The Wild Hunt's over, you son of a bitch, and you got bagged."

Bolan took the lead back toward the staircase. There was no one living between them and escape.

Grimaldi joined them at the front of the building. Four bodies were scattered around the entrance, and the pilot was bleeding from a scalp wound that didn't look serious.

They ran to the Mitsubishi 3000GT as the first Mexican police jeep rocked to a stop in front of the warehouse. The officer in the passenger seat shouted in Spanish for them to stop, then opened up with his revolver when they didn't.

Bolan slid behind the wheel and keyed the ignition. Two other Mexican police vehicles attempted to block his escape. Relying on the sports car's performance and raw power, he suddenly reversed and backed away. Less than fifty yards away, he made an outlaw U-turn and put the hammer down, going through the five forward gears in rapid succession. When he looked in the rearview mirror moments later, the spinning colored lights were in the near distance, and fading fast.

One hand on the wheel, the warrior lifted the mobile phone and punched in one of the numbers he had for the Farm.

Price answered on the first ring. "We got it, Striker. What wasn't in the computers at the warehouse, we were able to put together from the files Akira salvaged."

"Where's Thone?"

"Austria. I've got a military jet standing by in El Paso, and I've got a team of blacksuits from the Farm that can help with the final assault. It's going to be cutting it close, but I think I can get you to Austria by daybreak, at roughly the same time the President's due to arrive in Jerusalem after a stopover in Paris."

"Good enough."

14

Miami, Florida

"The man's a killer. I'm not cutting him loose."

Carl Lyons glared across the cluttered expanse of Sheriff Albert Hunesacker's desk. Behind the heavyset man with the florid face, through the room's only window, sandwiched between cheap copies of portraits of John F. Kennedy and John Wayne, the Able Team warrior could see the full dark of night sitting harsh over the city.

Lyons's frustration level had already been exceeded. He'd been on a paper chase inside the building for the past forty-five minutes but hadn't been able to locate Brognola. Each time he'd cornered someone, they'd kicked him upstairs. Hunesacker was as high as he could go and stay within Dade County.

"Look," Lyons said gruffly, "I didn't come down here tonight to get into a pissing contest with you. I'm here to take custody of Harold Brognola, and I mean to do it damn soon."

"The man was booked into my place of business, son," the sheriff said, "for a crime committed in my county. I don't hold with letting guilty parties go. Especially when they been here ventilating peace officers." He wrapped sausage-thick fingers over his potbelly and glared back.

Lyons reached inside his jacket and produced the papers Price had sent down by courier. "That's a writ for the release of Brognola." He tapped it with a forefinger. "And that's the presidential seal."

"It doesn't cut any ice with me," Hunesacker said. "This is a state matter. Those papers are federal. They don't apply."

"Can I borrow your phone?" Lyons asked, then stepped around the desk and picked up the receiver. After checking with a number he'd written on a card, he activated the speakerphone function.

It was answered on the first ring. "Yes." The man's voice was tense and irritated.

"Justice Agent Lambert here," Lyons said. "I'm here with the sheriff. I'm being generous by simply saying he's not being cooperative." He turned to the sheriff. "You know the governor's voice, of course."

"Goddamn it, Albert, give him his man and get the hell out of the way. I've already talked to three senators and four state representatives tonight. They've all vouched for Brognola."

"That's not how I'm in the habit of doing my job."

"It is tonight. Unless you'd like to make your fishing hobby a vocation after this term. Am I getting through to you?"

"Yeah."

"Then I expect to get to bed now and not be interrupted any more." The phone connection clicked dead.

Hunesacker reached into the top desk drawer and retrieved a big ring of keys. "Let's go get him."

Following the sheriff, Lyons walked a half step behind and to the right. Blancanales, his shoulder in a sling, and Schwarz met them in the foyer, then fell into the abbreviated parade.

Hunesacker led them to the elevator. They got off and Lyons read the information placards. "This goes to general lockup," he said.

"Yeah," Hunesacker replied. "That's where he is."

"He's a cop, for God's sake," Lyons bellowed. "If some of the hardcases you've got locked up in there found that out, they'd be all over him like a cheap suit."

"The story's been all over the television news," Blancanales said. "They'd recognize him."

"How long has he been there?" Lyons asked. They walked through a progression of narrow corridors until they reached the first checkpoint. The electronic gate whirred back on tracks and they passed through.

"A couple hours," Hunesacker said. "It took awhile to get him through processing. We didn't want to lose this one because of improper procedure."

Lyons felt a chill thrill through him. He wondered if Brognola was even still alive. It was easy to picture the big Fed lying quietly on a bed, an ice pick shoved through his larynx, courtesy of someone Thone had managed to slip into the system.

The general lockup was for most overnighters: drunks, vagrants and people waiting to be officially charged. Since Brognola was still waiting for a preliminary court appearance to discuss the murder charges, technically he numbered in those ranks.

It was a huge cage framed by steel bars, filled out by benches and a few cots hanging from the walls. Almost thirty men were inside, a mixture of races and crimes.

Hal Brognola sat on one of the bottom cots, his back against the wall and his left eye nearly swelled shut. A cut pulled at his lower lip. The other prisoners were giving him a wide berth.

Two men lay on the top bunk with their arms tossed over each other. Another was lying under Brognola's bunk, the fingers of one hand bent in an assortment of directions.

"Brognola," the sheriff called out, waving two uniformed jailers away from the cage.

The big Fed looked up, then saw the men of Able Team and got to his feet. Though disheveled and unshaved since morning, he adjusted his jacket and tie as he approached.

"You okay?" Blancanales asked.

"Yeah. Am I out of here, or just going for a visit?"

"Out."

"Terrific." Brognola turned to Hunesacker. "Amusing jail you've got here, Sheriff." He reached into his jacket pockets and removed a switchblade, brass knuckles and a Raven Arms .25 automatic. "Never a dull moment." He dropped the assortment of weapons into the sheriff's hands. "By the way, the guy under the cot is dead. He had the gun. I gave him one of the bullets back before I could get it away from him. The two clowns on the top cot need medical attention, but it's nothing permanent."

Before the sheriff could reply, he strode away from the holding tank.

Blancanales passed him a cigar.

"If I get lost finding my way out of here," Brognola said as the elevator dropped, "correct me."

"Right," Lyons replied. He'd always had respect for the Stony Man liaison over the years, but it had gone up tonight.

"Tell me what's going on with Thone."

"You can scratch Alexander De Moray," Lyons replied. "Striker caught up with him in Juarez at the alter-programming center. Using the computer records they swiped from the computers there, and cross-referencing them with ones from Clay Pigeons that Akira reconstructed, they tracked Thone to an ancestral castle in Austria. He did a paper jive with the ownership of the castle, made it look like it had been sold back in the late 1970s."

"But he'd retained ownership of it?"

"Yeah." Lyons went on full alert as they left the building and stepped out to the parking lot. Lamps threw a white glare over the dark asphalt.

"That's thin." Brognola thrust the unwrapped cigar between his teeth.

"It was," Blancanales agreed, "until the Bear located the Swiss accounts with banking accounts open in Innsbruck in Thone's name. The past twenty-four hours, Thone's been liquidating his assets here in the States—as much as he could of the ones that aren't being frozen—and had them moved to the Swiss accounts."

"He's there?" Brognola asked.

"Yeah," Schwarz answered. "Barb and Aaron confirmed it through satellite recon." He peeled his shirtsleeve back and checked his watch. "Striker and a blacksuit team should be there any minute now."

"What about Phoenix?"

"They're covering the President in Jerusalem."

"When is that going down?"

"Right about now," Lyons answered as he put his hand on the door of the Range Rover they'd driven in.

Without warning, rubber shrilled, coming closer as an engine shrieked in protest. Glancing to his right, Lyons saw a Chevy Blazer rocketing toward them. Breaking out their side arms, Blancanales and Schwarz returned fire against the truck full of gunners.

The Blazer swept by on its first pass. Bullets chopped holes in vehicles near the Range Rover and the Rover itself. Glass shattered out of the windows. Attorneys and clients and uniformed deputies took cover on the building's steps.

Certain that Brognola and his teammates were out of danger for the moment, Lyons raced to the back of the Range Rover. He threw the doors open and yanked open the equipment case holding an Armbrust antitank weapon.

Carrying a 67 mm warhead, the Armbrust was capable of taking out tank armor at three hundred yards. The Blazer was little over seventy yards away, swinging wide as the driver navigated the turn at the end of the parking lot, getting ready to come back for a second pass.

Settling the Armbrust onto his shoulder, Lyons jogged into the open and found target acquisition as the Blazer leaped forward again. He let out half his breath and squeezed the trigger. The 67 mm warhead sped true, crossing the distance in a heartbeat and impacting against the Blazer's front end.

The vehicle stopped dead in its tracks and flipped sideways, becoming a flaming mass of twisted wreckage. No one appeared to have survived.

Lyons dropped the Armbrust back into the Range Rover.

"Poor sons of bitches," Schwarz said as he opened the door. "They didn't know the Ironman. They didn't know they were bringing pistols and assault rifles to a cannon fight."

"We were here to get Hal," Lyons said as he clambered behind the wheel and keyed the ignition, "and I didn't intend to come in second place."

"I can appreciate that," the big Fed said as he gazed at the burning 4WD. "Let's get back to the Farm. Between you and me, I think we've about worn out our welcome in Miami for a while."

Jerusalem

THRONGING CROWDS gathered on both sides of Ruppin Street.

Seated in the black Cadillac fronting the limousine that carried the President of the United States, Yakov Katzenelenbogen surveyed the treacherous route the procession was taking. Hundreds of people, Israelis, Muslims,

Christians, natives, tourists and media personnel, had turned out hoping to see history in the making.

The Phoenix Force commander shifted uncomfortably in the seat. The lightning attacks on the Palestinian terrorist splinter groups had gone on throughout the night. There hadn't been time for sleep, and only brief respite for rest and meals.

For the Jerusalem visit, the President was leaving his security in the hands of his Secret Service, coordinating information through CIA intermediaries. Phoenix Force was operating as a wild card.

Katz listened to the standard checks through the radio frequency, using mental discipline to not allow them to become part of the background noise. Though the sweltering heat was broken somewhat by a cool wind drifting in from the Mediterranean Sea, the Israeli felt sorry for the Secret Service men and women standing post on the dust-covered limousine.

The small U.S. flags jutting up from the front and rear fenders of the limousine whipped in the wind. Moving at a sedate speed, the big luxury car made an easy target. A dozen Secret Service personnel trotted on both sides of the vehicle, one hand touching it at all times.

Cameramen from American stations surged in at Katz and he turned from the window. Israeli militia, augmented by UN troops, worked to keep the onlookers behind the yellow cords linked by red-and-white sawhorses.

The attack came without warning, from a direction not entirely anticipated.

Katz saw the pair of small Bell helicopters lift off from the south. Instantly his mind reasoned that the terrorists had somehow managed to bring them close on flatbed trailers without being caught. They were hundreds of meters away and closing fast when the Phoenix Force leader accessed the headset and alerted his team.

Using his hook, Katz opened his door and bailed out, sprinting for the President's limousine as he drew the SIG-Sauer 9 mm pistol from shoulder leather. An M-16/M-203 combination hung from his shoulder. "Get him out of the car!" he roared. "Now!"

At first the Secret Service agents were slow to react, not understanding the threat. One of the men moved to block Katz off, drawing his side arm and taking a defensive stance.

Then a rocket leaped from the pod at the skid of the lead helicopter, overshooting its target and impacting with a deafening crescendo in the landscaping near the Knesset. A crater opened up in the greensward, and dirt rained over the crowd.

"Oh, shit," the Secret Service agent said as he turned to the limousine. The big car braked to a stop, unable to even attempt evasive maneuvers inside the constricted area.

The thunder of the helicopters flashed by overhead, drowned out by the explosions of five other rockets that slammed into the ground around Ruppin Street. Tremors shook the earth.

"Calvin," Katz called out.

"Here," James responded. "I'm on them."

Even over the incredible noise created by the choppers and the echoes of the rockets, the loud boom of the Barrett .50-caliber sniping rifle was recognizable. The choppers turned and prepared for another pass.

Breaking through the line at the side of the street, Katz spotted four terrorists who opened up on Israeli militia. He fired from the point into their midst, running through a full clip in the SIG-Sauer as he took up position beside a news van anchored to the ground by hydraulic-powered external supports.

The terrorists went down as Katz's bullets and rounds from UN guns found their marks.

Leathering his side arm, Katz hit the transmit button,
"David. Gary. Rafael."

The rest of the team answered back in quick succession.
James's sniper rifle continued to bang out from his position atop an office building near the Knesset.

"They've got ground troops in the area, as well," Katz
said.

"Roger, Yakov. We've already spotted a few of them."

Scrambling, buffeted by people fleeing for their lives,
Katz climbed up the side of the news van. Once on top, he
flattened himself along the roof and took up the M-16/M-
203. He concentrated on the pair of helicopters, blinking
against the harsh sunlight that turned them into two-
dimensional black cutouts.

A rocket streaked from the pod and struck the stalled
limousine, ripping open the top and starting a fire inside.

Abruptly the lead helicopter started streaming black
smoke from the tail rotor. Katz had a brief impression of
the pilot being hit just before the big Barrett banged again.
Out of control, the helicopter slammed into the ground
near the Greek Monastery of the Cross.

Judging the distance as the surviving helicopter began a
sweeping turn to the east behind the Knesset, Katz slid a
finger into the M-203's trigger guard. Choosing his moment, he squeezed off the round. The rifle bucked against
his shoulder.

The 40 mm grenade covered the distance rapidly. On
target, it smashed against the Plexiglas bubble, which im-
ploded, killing the pilot and copilot. A few seconds later
the aircraft thudded into Ruppin Street, taking out one of
the official vehicles that had been abandoned.

Maintaining his position atop the news van, Katz used
the assault rifle on selective fire, carefully picking his targets in the confusion below. In seconds, the terrorists had
been beaten down.

After slipping a fresh clip into the M-16, the Phoenix Force leader tapped the transmit button. "Gary." Manning had been assigned to watch over the President in the confusion.

"He's safe," the Canadian reported. "The Secret Service got him into one of the buildings."

Tiredly Katz glanced to the east, past the wreckage of the cars and the helicopters, and found a promise of peace in the morning. Only the threat of the Foxglove alters remained. And he knew the Executioner was already in motion against Hayden Thone.

15

Austria

Watching the television in the bedroom in stony silence, Thone saw the replay of the last helicopter exploding in Jerusalem. Anger seized him, and he threw his glass into the fireplace. The alcohol left among the shards flamed to brief life and was gone.

"They're better than you thought," Mancuso stated.

"I've lost nearly everything in the past twenty-something hours," Thone snarled, "and all you can tell me is that these bastards are good?"

"They got De Moray and the Juarez plant," the Sicilian pointed out. "They took down Clay Pigeons and your military shipment connections. You should be grateful you're still alive and still free at this point."

Even hearing Mancuso say it didn't make the events seem real or even possible. He didn't know how the covert force had uncovered so much, hurt him so badly, and managed to save Brognola so quickly.

Thone paced the floor, then crossed the room to the phone. "There's still the Foxglove alters." He lifted the receiver and punched in the number to the message service he used to contact the dozens of Huntsman alters he'd created over the years and moved into positions of power in various terrorist groups.

Instead of the message he usually got, a stranger's voice said, "You haven't reached this recording in error, Thone. You're out of business, and the butcher's bill is due." Without warning, the connection broke.

Thone stared at the dead receiver. "They know about the Foxglove alters, too, and have intercepted the relay number."

"Hayden." Mancuso stood at the window where dawn had just turned the skies pink and gold. "We're under attack."

Turning cold inside, Thone approached the window and looked up at the two dozen parachutes that littered the sky, punching white holes in the tender pastels of the dawn. In spite of his financial setbacks, he was suddenly made aware of what he had left to lose.

"Let's go," he said. Even though the covert strike team had managed to track him down, he still had his contacts, and he could find a new way to activate the Foxglove alters.

MACK BOLAN THREW HIMSELF from the belly of the C-130 Hercules. The cold air cut into his face like edged icicles, and his goggles fogged over when he breathed out. Glancing back to the east, he saw the first of the group of blacksuits Price had sent, their white parachutes looking like mushrooms, lost periodically against the white expanse of the snow-covered mountain range.

The first unit was ground deployment to secure the perimeter and provide backup. A half dozen snowmobiles had been kicked out with them. One of them had gotten hung up in a tree, the chute lying like a shroud over the branches. A two-man team was already in motion on the ground to free it.

Bolan tapped the headset's transmit button. "Snowcat Leader, this is Striker."

"Go, Striker."

"When you people are in position, I want to know about it."

"Affirmative."

Checking his wrist altimeter, Bolan yanked the rip cord. With an audible crack, the rectangular-shaped canopy blossomed overhead. He gathered the shroud lines and altered his direction, aiming himself at the castle. The final shadows of the night hadn't yet left the castle grounds or the sprinkling of woods on the west side of the mountain.

Bolan used the headset again. "Sniper team."

They responded with a series of quick "Yes, sirs."

"When you're on the ground, start taking your targets down. We're not exactly coming in unannounced. Wolfpack Leader, split your teams as soon as you're on the ground and let's start claiming real estate."

"Yes, sir."

The Executioner tucked himself up into a parachutist's roll as he touched down inside the outer bailey. Unsnapping the chute, he dived behind a retaining wall that kept the terraced land from washing away through erosion.

Bullets from gunners taking cover at the castle's inner gatehouse ripped through the snow and scattered thick, black dirt. More of the Fortress Arms hardmen were sprinkled along the walkway of the outer curtain wall.

Bolan ripped out of the jumpsuit. He wore Hi-Risk Modular Armor, and had chosen as his distance weapon a Galil assault rifle chambered in 7.62 mm and equipped with an M-203 grenade launcher.

Slipping a 40 mm fragmentation grenade into the M-203, he leaned above the terraced slope just long enough to get target acquisition on the double doors of the inner gatehouse. He squeezed the trigger, then shifted quickly and picked off two riflemen on the curtain-wall walkways as the 40 mm warhead exploded against the doors.

He loaded an HE round and hit the gatehouse door again. This time they exploded off their hinges and leaned haphazardly inside the structure.

Tapping the transmit button, the warrior said, "Wolfpack Leader, I need two men to follow me into the gatehouse."

Wolfpack Leader assigned Wolfpack Three and Wolfpack Eight. Both men crossed the outer bailey at a run to join the Executioner.

Charges set at the outer gatehouse thundered and ripped the gates away. Seconds later, the first of the snowmobiles roared through the opening.

Bullets chopped into the ground near Bolan. He rolled, finding the sniper on the walkway, settled in behind cover so that only his hands and face showed. Coming to a rest on his stomach, the Executioner located the man through his scope, settled the cross hairs on him and squeezed the trigger.

The dead man toppled from the castle wall.

Gathering his feet, Bolan pushed himself into a run. It was less than sixty yards to the inner gatehouse, and he covered the distance in seconds.

No one else was inside the gatehouse. The Executioner didn't break stride as he plunged through and made for the keep. The doors were locked when he reached them.

Opening his chest pack, he took out a preshaped C-4 plastique charge and slapped it in the center of the door. He waved the two blacksuits back, then triggered the detonator. The explosion was more than was necessary, and the large, ornate door became kindling.

Whirling around the stone door frame, Bolan took the lead, holding the Galil before him in both hands. Three men were in the great hall, scrambling for position. The Executioner and the blacksuits opened up at once, withering fire on full-auto that scythed through their opponents.

Breath harsh and hot against the back of his throat now, Bolan charged up the curving stairs that led to the second floor. The Stony Man computer teams had been able to get their hands on the blueprints of the castle, and the warrior knew Thone's personal quarters were on the third floor.

He sprinted off the landing, running for the opposite end of the walkway to get to the other staircase, passing the door of a room where four of the castle guards were gathered. He pointed to the room without breaking stride, shouted, "Grenade," and fired the Galil from the hip as another armed man suddenly stepped out ahead of him.

The grenade went off as the heavy 7.62 mm round punched the man from the walkway over the railing.

At the next stairway, the warrior took the steps two and three at a time, ignoring the painful stitch that had started in his side. He turned right at the landing, rounding a sharp corner and finding himself suddenly face-to-face with three men. Holding the Galil like a bar in front of him, he launched himself into the group before they could move.

He caught the first man with a short butt stroke to the temple that took him out of the play. Then he was rolling free of the tangle of arms and legs. Coming up on his knees, he brought the assault rifle to his shoulder and fired.

The bullet crunched into the farthest man who'd brought his pistol to bear and knocked him up against the wall. The surviving gunner's weapon chipped stone splinters from the floor near Bolan's knees. Another round from the Galil removed him from the action.

The headset buzzed. "Striker, this is Wolfpack Leader."

"Go, Wolfpack Leader."

"We control the outer and inner baileys."

"The resistance?"

"They're not interested in putting up much of a fight now that they've realized we're here to stay."

"Then find Thone, and let me know when you do."

"Yes, sir."

Bolan paused at the side of the door to the Fortress Arms CEO's private quarters. He tried the knob and found it unlocked. Kicking the door open, he stepped inside the room, aware from the feeling he got that it was empty.

Crossing to the big windows at the back of the room, the warrior found himself in a position to look out over the western crest of the mountain just in time to note the four men skiing toward it.

He glanced down and saw one of the inner curtain walls twenty feet away and one floor down. Slinging the Galil over his shoulder, he took out the collapsible grappling hook and nylon cord. He made the cast easily and set the hook. As he tied the free end of the cord to the window frame over his head, he told the man nearest him, "Radio this in to Wolfpack Leader and see if they can get a couple snowmobiles out in pursuit."

"Yes, sir."

The warrior ripped one of the curtains away, flipped it over the nylon cord and leaped out. Instantly he slid along the cord, dropping as he crossed the distance. His legs absorbed the shock when he hit the inner curtain wall. Recovering quickly, he clambered up to the walkway and shouted to the man still inside Thone's quarters, "Cut the rope!"

A blade gleamed in the man's fist, then the rope went slack.

The warrior gathered it up and sprinted for the outer wall. In the distance, the four skiers had topped the ridge.

Kneeling, the Executioner unlimbered the Galil, settled the barrel on one of the stone wall projections, found a target in the scope and squeezed the trigger.

The flat crack of the rifle in the open echoed across the mountain range. A heartbeat later, the rearmost figure dropped in the snow. The other three men disappeared over the ridge.

Bolan used the grappling hook a final time to drop to the ground. Though fatigued and winded, he summoned his final reserves of strength and made himself run. Once he reached the man he'd killed, he freed him from the skis, fitted the toe bindings to the lip of his combat boots and headed out in pursuit of Thone.

At the crest, he looked down. The slope was broken, smooth and steep in places. He spotted Thone, eighty yards away and poling for the wooded area.

Bolan took up the Galil and settled on the two other men, unable to get a shot at the Fortress Arms CEO. He fired twice and both men went down. The way they fell suggested they weren't wearing body armor.

Slinging the Galil, the warrior pushed off. The snow shushed in his ears, and the reflected light was almost blinding. He pumped his arms hard and leaned into the slope, taking in every bit of speed he could.

For a moment he lost Thone because of a rise. When he came over it, he spotted the man through the underbrush, his neon blue snowsuit making him clearly visible. The Executioner understood the man's stance, knew that Thone was firing at him. A small tree to his left was sheared in two by a high-powered rifle bullet. Cutting back in, throwing out a sheet of wet snow, Bolan dropped to the ground for cover. Hayden Thone had been an Olympic medalist in skiing and shooting events.

"Striker, this is Snowcat Leader."

"Go, Snowcat Leader." Bolan pulled himself to the edge of the rise and glanced down. Thone was moving again, speeding down the slope, veering away from the drop-off to his right.

"They've got a chopper in the air," Snowcat Leader said. "They put out two of my machines before we could react. It's coming toward your position."

"Acknowledged." Then Bolan felt the vibration of the helicopter's rotors beating the air. The sound thundered into his ears as it came over the crest, floating overhead like an aerial shark.

Thone took a swooping angle down the mountainside, clearly intent on making the helicopter near the bottom.

Glancing at the drop-off the Austrian had avoided, Bolan stood, released the toe bindings and pushed off, poling as hard as he was able. The drop-off came up suddenly and he felt like he was flying down the mountainside, the wind cutting into his face.

He scanned Thone's progress and knew he'd timed it right.

At the top of the drop-off, he saw that Thone had taken a stance and was waiting for him. The drop-off was roughly thirty feet straight down. He hoped that the snow was thick enough to cushion most of his fall as he shot out over the edge.

Thone was perhaps forty yards away, and Bolan knew he was bigger than any target the Austrian had ever practiced on. The only thing he had going for him was that Thone would be remembering that this target would be shooting back.

Airborne, arcing high, the Executioner kicked free of the skis so there'd be less chance of breaking his legs when he hit. He tucked himself into a ball and flipped, drawing the Desert Eagle as naturally as if he'd drawn a breath. It filled his hand as he swiveled his head and looked for

Thone. He spotted the man just as something smashed into the ceramic plate protecting his back. He lost his breath, but managed to turn so his gun arm was toward the Austrian.

Gravity reclaimed him and he started to fall. Another bullet struck him, this one burning across the top of his left shoulder.

He became a gun sight, not aware of gravity or fear. The Desert Eagle leaped in his hand as he fired it dry, concentrating on Thone's head beside the rifle butt. Then he smashed into the snowbank and lost sight of everything.

Lungs burning for oxygen, black comets swirling in front of his eyes, he pushed his way out of the snowbank and took a deep breath. Automatically he fed a fresh clip into the .44's butt.

Thone lay sprawled across the ground twenty feet away, blood spreading across the melting snow.

The helicopter hovered less than eighty yards away. Before it could take off, the Executioner leveled the big .44 Magnum pistol and fired the whole clip as fast as he could pull the trigger. Pieces of the tail rotor sheared off as the 240-grain bullets smashed into it.

Struggling like an ungainly duck, the chopper tried to gain altitude, then whirled out of control like a dervish and crashed into the trees.

Battered and bruised, Bolan limped toward the Fortress Arms CEO, recharging his weapon and holding it in front of him. He stood over Thone, not knowing how many of the .44 rounds had hit the man. But it had been enough.

He thought about the career in death and violence that Hayden Thone had carved out for himself from a business that had once reflected honor and duty. Arming a warrior to fight against his enemies was an honest trade, but fomenting death and destruction in its purest sense was nothing short of evil.

As long as laws existed to protect the meek and the mild and the hopes for a future filled with peace, there would be men who'd put themselves above those laws. And as long as the Executioner had one bloody mile left in him for his Everlasting War, he'd stand in the trenches and bury those men.

TAKE 'EM FREE
4 action-packed novels plus a mystery bonus
NO RISK
NO OBLIGATION TO BUY

Adventure and suspense in the
midst of the new reality

JAMES AXLER

DEATH LANDS®

Shadowfall

The nuclear conflagration that had nearly consumed the world
generations ago stripped away most of its bounty. Amid the ruins
of the Sunshine State, Ryan Cawdor comes to an agonizing
crossroads, torn by a debt to the past and loyalty to the present.

Hope died in the Deathlands, but the will to live goes on.